D0312437

LOVE BY DESIGN

LOVE BY DESIGN

•

Jenny Jacobs

AVALON BOOKS
NEW YORK

Published by Thomas Bouregy & Co., Inc.
160 Madison Avenue, New York, NY 10016

Library of Congress Cataloging-in-Publication Data

Jacobs, Jenny, 1965–
   Love by design / Jenny Jacobs.
        p. cm.
   ISBN 978-0-8034-9903-4 (acid-free paper)
  1. Women tailors—Fiction.   2. Single mothers—Fiction.
3. Interior decoration—Fiction.   4. Carpenters—Fiction.
I. Title

   PS3612.A94435L68   2008
   813'.6—dc22   2008005919

PRINTED IN THE UNITED STATES OF AMERICA
ON ACID-FREE PAPER
BY HADDON CRAFTSMEN, BLOOMSBURG, PENNSYLVANIA

For my daughter Jessica,
who has always been my biggest fan.

Chapter One

Tess Ferguson had never been to Michael Manning's workshop before but Greta—her sister-slash-boss—had given clear, precise driving directions. Not for the first time did Tess wonder why Greta thought this task was so important it couldn't wait a day or two. With Greta in the hospital, it was up to Tess to keep her sister's interior design business going, and this errand didn't seem like an urgent priority. But what Greta wanted, Greta got.

Tess parked in the gravel lot, spotted the plain, unremarkable sign on the metal building—MICHAEL MANNING, CARPENTER—and climbed out of her compact car, grabbing the folder of information and her bag from the seat beside her. He was going for the simple look, she thought, giving the building a once-over. Not trying to impress people with his posh surroundings. That would go over well in a Midwestern college town like this, still struggling with its transition from small town to small city, from farm roots to strip malls.

The spring sun was bright and warm on her face as she strode across the lot to the heavy glass door. She spotted a discreet sign printed with the words SHOW-ROOM HOURS: BY APPOINTMENT ONLY. She sighed and hitched her purse on her shoulder. Greta hadn't mentioned that little detail and Tess hadn't bothered to call ahead, but had taken advantage of an unexpected cancellation in her schedule to squeeze him in. Tess reached for the door anyway and found it unlocked. Surely that meant someone was around to help her.

The building's surprisingly attractive interior contrasted sharply with its unexceptional exterior. Subdued lighting, polished wood trim, and thick carpet warmed the space and made it feel welcoming. An arts-and-crafts-style desk standing just inside the front door drew her attention. Cluttered with sufficient papers and office supplies to mark it as a working desk and not a display model, it nevertheless begged to be touched. She ran a hand along the silky smooth top. She wouldn't mind having this in her own home.

She supposed the showroom assistant usually sat here but since showroom hours were by appointment only and she didn't have one, she could understand the assistant's absence. But now what was she going to do with the samples and specs she was supposed to deliver?

Her first impulse was to shout, "Anyone home?" but knowing how Greta would feel about that, Tess squelched the impulse.

She walked farther into the showroom, which was furnished like a house, with kitchen cabinetry here, living room furniture opposite, built-in bookshelves flanking a fireplace along that wall, a bedroom suite and bathroom vanity along another. Showing off his versatility, she guessed. She knew what kind of prices he charged and it looked like he earned them.

She found herself stopping every few feet to admire the elegant lines and the clean design, to touch the satiny finish of the pieces, imagining how they'd look in her home, replacing the battered yard sale finds and cheap build-it-yourself pieces that filled her side of the duplex she rented. Being creative, she'd spruced up her furniture with new paint and slipcovers and she'd felt satisfied, but looking at what Michael Manning had created, she found herself lusting for good quality, well-designed pieces that she wouldn't have to hide behind fabric and paint. She told herself that when her daughter, Belinda, was a little older and not so hard on things, she could invest in better pieces. Maybe by then she'd have a few extra dollars to finance the acquisition.

Hearing the whine of a power saw, Tess decided her best bet was to follow the sound to its source. She located it down one showroom aisle, behind a set of swinging metal doors. A sign over the double doors said EMPLOYEES ONLY.

Ignoring the sign as she ignored most signs, she pushed one of the doors open, then peered inside. Here was a different world: bright fluorescent lighting, utilitarian metal shelving towering overhead, stacks of plywood and laminate slotted into racks, sawhorses holding up lengths of wood, workstations littered with power tools scattered across the vinyl floor, sawdust everywhere. She sneezed.

On the right, another set of double doors led—she guessed from what Greta had told her—to the finish room where furniture would be stained or painted, then crated for shipment and delivery. On the left, a half-open door revealed a computer on a desk—probably the owner's office.

At the back of the workshop near the rear delivery doors, she spotted a young man with his shirt off running an enormous circular saw, ripping a thick panel of plywood, oblivious to her standing there. Wearing ear protection, he couldn't hear her. How could she get his attention without startling him and making him lose a thumb?

As she debated her next move, the finish room doors burst open and a rangy man in work boots, dusty jeans, and a sweat-soaked T-shirt strode through. He caught sight of Tess and switched direction, coming toward her. She stared, spellbound. He was the best thing she had seen in a long, long time: tall and lean with an attractive, expressive face. Heat and strength radiated from him. She wanted to draw the angular planes of his face, try to capture the play of light and shadow.

"I'm from Interiors," Tess said when the man reached her. He smelled intoxicating: soap and clean laundry, hard work and wood shavings.

"Got that Weatherhill stuff for me?" he asked cheerfully, raising his voice to be heard over the sound of the circular saw. Which meant he must be Michael, and her heart sank.

He requires handling, Greta had said, but she hadn't specified the nature of the handling he required. Tess now suspected that she'd misunderstood Greta's warning. She'd assumed Greta meant that he was temperamental and difficult to get along with, but meeting him in person, she didn't think that was the problem. He didn't give the impression of being volatile, mercurial. He gave the impression of being calm and strong and capable. So what had Greta meant? Greta's warnings weren't lightly given, and if she said Michael required handling, then he did. Tess backed up half a step as he drew nearer, big and warm. She wished she'd pressed Greta on the question. It suddenly seemed important to know.

"Yes," she said finally, gathering her scattered wits. She didn't ordinarily let men throw her for a loop, not even attractive, calm men; maybe especially not attractive, calm men. She sucked in a breath and confirmed a little breathlessly, "The Weatherhill stuff."

"Let's get out of here," he said, again raising his voice

over the noise. "Jimmy's on a roll and I don't think he's going to turn off that saw anytime soon." He stomped the dust from his boots on the rubber mat by the doors before leading her back into the showroom. The door swung shut behind them, muffling the sound of the saw.

"Let's take a look," he said, walking over to the desk Tess coveted at the front of the showroom. He pulled a chair around for her and waited until she sat before taking his own seat. Polite too. What did Greta have against him?

Tess handed him the folder and he opened it without comment. She watched as he bent over his task and noticed his thick sandy hair was a tad long. The too-long hair didn't quite go with his air of control and discipline. He didn't strike her as the type who was too impatient to bother with a haircut. On the contrary, he seemed calm and unhurried. The lack of hurry was part of the discipline. It was more like he hadn't happened to notice his hair had gotten so long it had started to curl near his collar. Obviously he didn't have a wife or a girlfriend to remind him.

That's enough, she told herself sternly. *He's a subcontractor.* Then she grinned at herself. That was exactly the kind of thing Greta would say.

His angular face looked drawn, like he'd seen it coming but hadn't gotten out of the way fast enough, the square jaw just pugnacious enough for her to think that next time he'd have a better response. A quicker one, anyway. To whatever it had been.

When he glanced up at her, she found herself looking into the saddest brown eyes she'd ever seen. She'd looked into a lot of sad eyes in her life—witness the three dogs with whom she and her daughter shared their duplex. They wouldn't have gotten in if they'd been frolicsome puppies with fire in their eyes. Everyone loved frolicsome puppies with fire in their eyes. They didn't need Tess to rescue them. But first Rufus and then Mooch and then Agnes had looked up as she passed by and fixed her with their depthless sad eyes that seemed to say, *You're going to leave me here too, aren't you? You're going to pick one of the fat, innocent puppies, the ones who don't know, so that you can look at them and smile and pretend you don't know either.*

But I do know, Tess had thought and now she had Rufus and Mooch and Agnes living in her house, and they didn't look so sad anymore. They didn't look fat and innocent, either. Knowing, that was it. Wise. They had seen it all clearly and now they knew enough to appreciate a bowl of food and a warm place in the sun.

But these were the saddest eyes she had ever seen, and they didn't belong to a dog she could bring home. Michael smiled at her from across the desk and even though the smile was warm and genuine, it didn't change the sadness in his eyes.

Requires handling, Tess thought. Well, darn it. Couldn't Greta have been a little more specific in her warning? If she had been, Tess would've arrived here with her armor intact. No more strays, she'd vowed.

The last one, a down-on-his-luck poet, had stolen her checkbook and cleaned out her account, leaving Tess and her daughter with nothing. Tess couldn't even pay the rent. She couldn't risk a mistake like that again. When it was just her, it was all right to misjudge someone. But she had Belinda to look after now, and she couldn't take foolish risks anymore—not with her heart, and certainly not with her wallet.

Not that she thought Michael Manning would be dangerous to her wallet. Oh, no. Her instinct was to bring him home and feed him and hug him for as long as it took to drive the sadness away. Her standard remedy for strays. Stray-tending 101. No wonder Greta had kept her away from him for so long.

"Your furniture is beautiful," she blurted out. "The lines are so graceful. I can see the patience it took to make each piece and the pleasure you had in making it." A betraying blush rose on her cheeks as she spoke. The words were heartfelt but she should know by now to tone her reactions down.

Michael didn't seem to notice her discomfort. He said, "Thank you. I enjoy my work," and then he turned back to the samples and specs she'd given him.

He was building a settee to match the antique living room set one of Greta's clients had inherited. The antique sofa had been unsalvageable, with springs sprung and the frame falling to pieces, but Greta had promised a reproduction that would match the other antiques in the set and hold up to everyday wear.

"This is going to look awful in Marla Weatherhill's living room," Michael said finally, a small smile on his face as he set the folder aside. The husky timbre of his voice sent a shiver of goose bumps along her arms.

"Isn't it just?" she agreed. How soon could she get out of here? And would it be before or after she did something regrettable? Fortunately, her voice too, was calm and a little amused as she spoke. "They've got that badly designed contemporary split with all that track lighting. Heavy antiques will look terrible in there." She indicated a photo of the house in the folder. As she pointed, her hand brushed his. The feel of his skin, warm and electric, alerted her senses. Uh-oh. With a jolt, she glanced up. Didn't he feel that? His face was calm and impassive. Apparently not.

"They wouldn't listen to Greta?" he asked.

"The furniture is very meaningful to Frank," Tess said, frowning. There was a subtext to the conversation but she was the only one who noticed it. How very very irritating. "I suspect Marla is hoping a freak tornado destroys it all while it's still in storage," she added.

"What's Greta doing?"

"Painting the walls a rich cream. Tones down the contemporary feel—all those dazzling white walls are a little much. But she wants to keep the walls light enough so the place won't resemble a cave. I'm doing toile curtains in this print." She fingered the swatch in the folder. She itched to design a toile herself, picturing American pioneer activities instead of the usual French pastoral scene, but it was hard to devote time to projects that had little hope of coming to fruition. "This gives an impression of being antique but isn't heavy. Then only a few choice accessories to draw the eye around the room and balance the darkness and heaviness of the furniture. Plus tons of flowers."

"Flowers are good."

"My idea," Tess said. "Bowls of bright fresh flowers make any room look better. We just have to get Marla to write that final check somehow."

"That's the truth. You said you're making the curtains?"

"Yes."

"Then you're Greta's seamstress."

"And all around gofer, yes."

"I thought her sister was her seamstress." Michael's brows drew together, perplexed.

"I am her sister."

Now he looked surprised. "You're not what I expected."

"We don't look anything alike," Tess said, assuming his comment referred to her obvious physical differences from Greta.

"That's not what I meant," Michael said. "The way Greta talks about you . . ." His voice trailed off as if he suddenly realized the trap.

"How does she talk about me?" Tess demanded. Greta and Michael had been talking about her? Why on earth? As far as she knew, Greta didn't have talks with any of her other clients about Tess. *She'd better not,* Tess thought, outraged.

"Like you're considerably tougher than she is," Michael said, his expression showing his reluctance to explain. But of course after a comment like that, Tess wasn't going to let him get away with not explaining. He hesitated, as if debating the wisdom of his next words, then said, "She looks up to you. She didn't mention how nice you are."

"Huh," Tess said. He must have gotten confused by a remark Greta made. Greta couldn't possibly look up to Tess. And what was this about *nice*? When had *nice* ever been an adequate adjective to describe Tess?

"Greta says you're a take-no-prisoners kind of person," he said, giving her a slow smile. The slow smile nearly made her heart stop beating. "She was pretty sure we'd never get along."

"Huh," Tess said again, narrowing her eyes at the comment. "That's very interesting."

Michael watched her go, the heavy glass showroom door swinging shut behind her, leaving the room a whole lot less interesting than it had been before. He caught his breath, feeling as if she'd stolen the oxygen from the room when she left. *That* was Greta's sister? From Greta's description, he'd pictured a sturdy matron who could benchpress a Volvo, suffered from a short temper, and enjoyed conflict. Which he definitely did not. Calm, that was what he wanted. Peace. He might not be happy but at least he didn't spend all his time arguing these days.

Theresa—Greta called her by a nickname he couldn't remember at the moment, but he knew her name was Theresa—had been smaller than he'd expected. Greta had implied something in the neighborhood of an Amazon. That wasn't quite right, he realized, though now he understood Greta's description better. Despite her small stature, Theresa had exuded strength and determination, a presence that gave you the impression that she was bigger than she was. He had no doubt she could handle herself and anyone who might cross her path, but not in the way Greta had implied.

Also, Greta had failed to mention how pretty Theresa was. All those dark curls framing the sharp angles of her face: high cheek bones, strong jaw, full red lips curving into a big smile, flashing black eyes. She reminded him of a gypsy. He wasn't in the market for gypsies, he reminded himself firmly, in case he tried to forget. He wasn't in the market for anyone.

Greta, he thought, picking up the folder and heading back to the workshop. *What are you up to?* He'd been fully prepared to deal with an impatient, fast-charging termagant but not the warm woman who was delighted by his work and open enough to tell him so. She'd taken him completely by surprise. He hadn't been prepared to respond to her so strongly. But he was going to crush that impulse. He wasn't interested. Not in Theresa, not in any woman. He had no interest in jeopardizing his hard-won peace by pursuing an attraction with a woman, especially one like Theresa. She definitely wasn't his type. *Greta* was his type, although he'd gently turned her down when she'd expressed interest a few years ago. She'd taken it with a smile and good grace and had never let it affect their working relationship.

He grinned at the memory. He couldn't imagine Theresa *not* letting something like that affect a working relationship. If he rejected her, she'd probably spit in his eye and stop referring clients to him. Not because she was impatient and hard-charging, as Greta claimed, but because she was passionate and wore her feelings close to the surface. That smoldering emotion wouldn't require much of a spark to flare and burn out of control.

He shook himself. It didn't matter. He planned to put the dark-haired gypsy directly out of his mind. That was precisely what he was going to do. He wasn't going to risk the peace of mind he'd battled to hard to create. He wasn't about to give up his contentment, his solitude, not for that black-eyed charmer. Not for anyone. So he was extremely irritated when Jimmy had to wave a hand in front of his face in order to get his attention.

"Slow down, you lunatic!" Greta's voice, sharp and angry, broke the silence.

Fairy godmother, Tess reminded herself, taking a deep breath and counting to ten. Then twenty. *No strangling my own fairy godmother.* She glanced at the speedometer: fifteen miles an hour.

"Dammit, Tess," her fairy godmother said, which Tess was pretty sure Walt Disney never would have allowed, no matter what the provocation. "Could you be more careful?"

"You know, you don't handle discomfort very well," Tess said to her sister. Pain and fatigue lined Greta's slender, fine-boned face and her usual sleek blond coif fell in frizzed tendrils around her face. "You could have stayed with us." *Us* was Tess and her eight-year-old daughter, Belinda, who required even more of Tess' energy than Greta did.

Holding the car door open for her sister, Tess looked up at Greta's tiny, renovated Victorian house on one of the few remaining brick-lined streets in downtown Lawrence, Kansas. It was the inevitable bumpy ride that sparked Greta's current complaint. Tess sighed as she calculated the distance to the front door. Not the most accommodating of homes in which to recover from major surgery.

"Stay with you? Are you kidding?" Greta said. "I'd give it two days before we stopped speaking to each other. Your place is too small. You may not have noticed, but I'm a little surly right now. Somehow I don't imagine having the dogs jumping up on me would improve my disposition any."

The dogs never jumped up on anyone, but Tess decided now was not the time for that conversation. And it probably wouldn't be prudent to agree about the surliness.

"How are you going to manage the steps without me?" Tess asked. Her own rental duplex was a one-story ranch-style house with no steps from the driveway. She opened her mouth to point this out, then took one look at the stubborn, set look on her sister's face and stopped arguing.

She helped Greta out of the car and then gave her a hand as she slowly and painfully maneuvered her way up the five steps to the front door. Tess knew the jarring on Greta's just-repaired knee wasn't doing her attitude or her injury any good, but Greta didn't make any comments, so neither did Tess. There was a flight of interior stairs up to Greta's bedroom—"the command center" from which she ran her successful business, Interiors— and those steeply pitched narrow stairs were what concerned Tess most.

She unlocked the light blue front door and pushed it open. She helped Greta, still awkward on her crutches, across the threshold. A few scary steps down the slick-tiled hallway and then Greta collapsed into a wing chair in the living room. Tess hustled to slide a hassock under her feet.

"Pain pill," Greta said, closing her eyes. "You drive like a maniac."

Fairy godmother, Tess reminded herself, going into the kitchen to get a glass of water so Greta could swallow her pills. If not for her sister, Tess and Belinda would be living on the streets. *That's what comes of trusting strays,* her mother had said. *What did you think would happen?* But Greta had come through. She always did, just like a fairy godmother.

Tess didn't have to remind herself to be grateful very often but now and then Greta pushed her hard enough that she had to repeat the phrase like a litany to keep from losing her temper. *Fairy godmother, fairy godmother, fairy godmother.*

Despite suffering an excess of family, Tess had learned as a young child that the only person she could truly count on was Greta. Beautiful, elegant Greta had always been the kind of child their parents could be proud of. Even so, she'd followed her own path, reaping success in every endeavor she undertook, because along with being beautiful and elegant, she was smart, savvy, and determined. Inelegant, earthy Tess, on the other hand, had caused her parents (as they routinely lectured her) nothing but heartache and misery—"and probably constipation too," Tess had once remarked to Greta. She followed her own path as well but not as successfully as Greta, for despite also being smart, savvy, and determined, she leaped before looking, spoke without thinking, and generally had a cheerful disregard for the consequences of her actions. Which was why she'd needed a fairy godmother to bail her out more than once.

She handed Greta the glass of water and the bottle of pain pills. Greta swallowed the capsules gratefully. She'd hurt her knee a few weeks before, during an early spring ski vacation with her then-beau, who handily disappeared shortly after their return from Colorado. Greta's injury required extensive reconstructive surgery, which in itself irritated her to no end ("I don't even like to ski that much"). Though Greta had just been discharged from the hospital, Tess had little doubt her sister would be back on her feet in no time, undaunted and probably stronger than before. Ready to tackle the double black diamond again next year, except that she'd sworn off skiing in a fit of pique. Greta's piques usually held firm.

Greta let out a gentle snore. Tess found a lightweight afghan and covered her with it. Then Tess sat down on the wing chair opposite her sister and rested her chin in her hand. This was going to be a long, long spring. April is the cruelest month, she remembered from English class, and though she was pretty sure the poet was talking about existential pain, not ski injuries and the aftermath thereof, she felt the sentiment captured her feelings exactly. Greta operating at full capacity was a challenge. Greta out of commission, even partially and temporarily, was a reason to think about picking up and moving to San Antonio. Or Maui. Somewhere a long way from this Midwestern college town.

She probably ought to hire a personal helper for Greta, though Greta would claim she didn't need it. And they really couldn't afford it. No one else in the family would lend a hand, Tess knew, a sigh escaping her lips. Jeanette and Todd had their own families to tend to and Cat had been gone a long time now. As usual, it was Tess and Greta against the world. But the world had gotten so much more complicated than it used to be.

Take care of yourself first. The words Belinda's pediatrician had said to Tess at their last visit echoed in her mind. *You're in this forever. This is never going away.* *This* being Belinda's cognitive impairment. "Retarded," they used to call it when Tess was in school. She liked the phrase "cognitively impaired" a lot better.

Tess looked at Greta, tucked under the afghan. Easy for the pediatrician to say. He didn't have to cope with Belinda's demands and now Greta's temporary incapacitation. Though Tess understood the purpose of the sentiment, she was frequently annoyed by the platitudes other people heaped on her. "Take care of yourself," they always said, without giving any concrete help, never having to back up their words with actions. "How?" Tess always wanted to demand. "So you'll be babysitting tonight?"

Chocolate, Tess thought, to calm herself down. She'd get extra chocolate for this. Greta had always been there for her. Time to return the favor, that was all. Next spring, they'd be laughing over this. That possibility seemed hard to imagine now.

Casting an eye at Greta's restless form, Tess reached for her shoulder bag and removed her sketchbook. She'd gotten clever at snatching moments here and there to work on her fabric designs and she took the opportunity now, her colored pencil flying beneath her fingers, the stress easing from her shoulders as she worked.

A few minutes later, Greta, roused from her nap, cleared her throat and blinked groggily at Tess. "Now I have a crick in my neck," she complained. A smile tugged at Tess' lips. *I've got a pain in the neck too,* she thought.

"Maybe we should get you upstairs," Tess said, though she didn't know how they were going to manage the steps. She ran a hand through her dark, slightly sweaty curls and wished she'd thought about renting a hospital bed and installing it on the ground floor. But even if she'd thought of it, she knew Greta would have refused the accommodation. Greta ran her successful business from "the command center" and a bed in the living room would never do. At least there was a bathroom upstairs. *There,* Tess told herself. *It could be worse.* She could be emptying chamber pots.

Greta took a deep breath and struggled out of the chair. Tess was there to offer a shoulder and the crutches. They staggered over to the staircase, where Greta smiled and said, "Watch this." She turned around and plunked herself down on the step. Keeping her injured leg extended—easy enough, since she was wearing a splint from thigh to ankle—she boosted her bottom to the next step up. Using the maneuver, she slowly made her way to the top. At the landing, she clumsily pushed off against the hallway wall until she achieved a standing position.

"Lacks elegance," Tess said, following her up the stairs, crutches in hand.

"Form follows function," Greta said, leaning heavily into Tess before wielding the crutches and making her way down the hall. Once in the bedroom, Tess helped her sister get into bed, then plumped pillows and smoothed the comforter around her.

"Hand me my laptop."

"You need rest."

Greta opened her mouth to protest but then she seemed to sink into the pillows. She closed her mouth again. A moment later, her eyes fluttered shut.

Tess made sure the phone, pain pills, and water were within reach, then leaned down and kissed Greta on the cheek.

"I'm going to pick up Belinda from school now," she whispered. "We'll be back with some dinner for you later."

Greta nodded without opening her eyes, and Tess left the room.

Tess found a smooth walnut serving tray in Greta's sleek, contemporary kitchen and put a bowl of warm vegetable soup and a slice of thick crusty bread from Wheatfield's on it, along with a glass of orange juice and one of the cloth napkins Greta preferred to use.

"Want one?" Belinda said, pointing to the tray. Tess smiled down at her daughter. Belinda's heart-shaped, fine-boned face was reminiscent of her birth mother's,

Tess' best friend from high school; her dark eyes and tight dark curls came from her father. Both had abandoned her, though in somewhat different ways. Tess' heart caught at the memory. How could you abandon such a lovely, sweet child? Belinda was the very best stray Tess had ever taken in, and if she had come at a high cost, then Tess didn't begrudge the price.

But no more strays, Tess reminded herself firmly, thinking of Michael's sad brown eyes. When she glanced down at Belinda again, her daughter's grin was so warm and her face so open and trusting that Tess dropped a kiss on her upturned nose before unearthing a second tray and arranging Belinda's chicken and french fries on it.

"I'll bring Greta's up first," she told Belinda.

"Why not mine?"

"Because you can wait twelve seconds."

"Uh-uh."

"Go up and tell Aunt Greta I'm bringing her dinner," Tess said, as if Greta might not have surmised that herself from the commotion they were making in the kitchen. Happily distracted, Belinda charged up the stairs and darted into Greta's bedroom.

"No jumping on Aunt Greta!" Tess warned, hurrying up the steps behind Belinda. "Don't hurt her bad knee!" When she got to the bedroom, Belinda was already ensconced on the big brass bed, snuggling with Greta.

"On Aunt Greta's good side," Belinda announced.

"Good planning," Tess said, depositing the tray on

Greta's lap. "I always try to stay on Greta's good side."

"Ha ha," Greta said sourly, taking a long swallow of juice. "I didn't think I was hungry but this smells delicious."

Tess drew the silk damask drapes closed and switched on the brass floor lamp that curved gracefully over the bed. Greta's room was luxurious and feminine without being girlish or froufrou. The French provincial dresser was matched with nightstands of the same style. A small white desk with gold trim sat under the window. Greta had commissioned Michael to make an office armoire that fit in with the style of the other furniture and hid the vulgar files, printer, and fax machine that Greta despised but needed to run the business. Whitewashed wainscoting covered the bottom half of the walls, while ivory wallpaper dotted with tiny red rosebuds covered the upper half. White painted crown molding and chair rail added the final touches.

Just being in the room made Tess feel cosseted and relaxed and she wasn't even on the king-size featherbed with its extra-soft mattress and profusion of velvet and satin pillows. It was easy to understand why Greta wasn't interested in setting up a regular office elsewhere in the house. If Tess had a sanctuary like this, she'd probably never leave it.

"Dinner?" Belinda asked.

"I'm getting it," Tess said. "Give me a minute, your highness."

"Belinda," the little girl corrected her, her sweet, delicate face a picture of seriousness.

"I know," Tess said, coming around to the other side of the bed to ruffle her fingers through her daughter's hair. "Anything else I can get you while I'm in the kitchen, Greta?" Greta shook her head, her mouth full of soup.

Downstairs, Tess took a minute to restore order to the kitchen, tossing trash and wiping counters, though not going so far as to sweep the floor. Then she grabbed the tray with Belinda's chicken and fries and headed upstairs again.

"Where's yours?" Greta asked when Tess came into the bedroom with Belinda's food.

"I'll fix something later," Tess said, handing the platter to Belinda, who scooted into a sitting position that precisely mimicked Greta's and placed the tray on her lap just as Greta had it on hers. "I'm not hungry at the moment."

"Are you on another diet?" Greta asked suspiciously, tearing off a hunk of crusty bread with her sharp white teeth. Belinda did exactly the same with a piece of chicken.

"No," Tess said. "I've accepted that I'll never have a teenage body again."

"Good. You look ridiculous skinny."

"Thank you," Tess said. "I think."

"You don't have the build for skinny. On the other

hand, I look like a Thanksgiving turkey if I put on two pounds." To Tess' knowledge, Greta hadn't gained an ounce since her high school days—unlike mere mortals such as Tess—so how she would know such a thing was impossible to say.

Belinda was watching them keenly. "Are you fat, Mama?" There was no judgment in her tone, just curiosity.

"No!" Greta said.

"Did someone tell you I was fat?" Tess demanded, then shook her head and said to Greta, "Finish your soup."

"Did we get that check—"

"Greta, you just had major surgery. Can't you take the day off work?"

"Not easily," Greta said. She finished the soup and handed the empty bowl to Tess. "At least tell me how today went."

"If it will get you to relax, okay," Tess said, setting Greta's tray and dishes on the dresser to take down to the kitchen later. "But we're not going to have a meeting now. No one is going to suffer because you're laid up. Except me. You're not in the rocket science business."

"*We,*" Greta said. "How hard is that to say? *We* are not in the rocket science business."

"It's your business."

"I would give you my right kidney," Greta said. "You think I'm going to quibble over who started the company? I couldn't run the place without you."

"Any competent twelve-year-old—"

"Shut up," Greta said, exasperation and pain making her less patient than usual.

"That's not polite," Belinda informed her.

Greta glanced over at her niece. "I have had this argument with your mother once a week for the last three years. I can tell her to shut up if I want to."

Belinda blinked and put a french fry in her mouth. Greta leaned over and kissed her cheek. "You're right, it's not polite."

"Say sorry."

"Tess, I'm sorry I told you to shut up," Greta said. Tess couldn't remember receiving a more insincere apology, not even from her rat of an ex-husband for cheating on her. At least he'd sounded like he'd meant it. Tess' interpretation of tone was confirmed when Greta added, "However, if you continue speaking in this vein, I won't answer for the consequences."

"My meeting with Michael was fine," Tess said, sensibly changing the subject as she gathered the remains of Belinda's meal to add to the pile of Greta's dishes. "You've always told me that he requires handling. I thought that you meant he was a prima donna. Or whatever the male version is."

"Prima don?" Greta offered. "That's not what I meant. He's not—how do I put this? You can't fix him, Tess."

"I can't fix anyone."

"That has never stopped you trying."

"You're a fine one to talk," Tess said. Then her eyes widened. "Aha. You tried."

"I've never been so courteously rejected in my life," Greta said, a rueful expression on her face as she made the admission. "Even though I know I'm just his type."

"What is it with men and the chilly blonde thing?"

"I am *not* chilly," Greta said in freezing tones.

"You bet," Tess said. "I promised Belinda she could watch a movie tonight but it's up to you whether she does it here or at home."

"Here is fine. I could use the distraction."

"It's going to be *Finding Nemo,*" Tess warned.

"I've watched that movie with Belle five hundred times," Greta complained, using her nickname for Belinda. "Look, kid, you gotta branch out a little. Would it kill you to take a look at *Monsters, Inc.*? Or a princess movie? What would be wrong with a princess movie?"

Of course a fairy godmother would be partial to princess movies, Tess thought with affection. She liked how Greta always treated Belinda as if she were just a regular little girl. Very few people did.

"*Finding Nemo,*" Belinda said in a tone that brooked no argument, crossing her arms and glaring at her aunt. "Nemo is a clown fish."

"I know, honey," Greta said.

"Saw a clown fish," Belinda said.

"Pet store," Tess explained.

"So that means this time next week you'll be setting up an aquarium," Greta predicted.

"Belinda and I have an understanding," Tess said.

"As long as we visit the pet store regularly, she doesn't actually require the adoption of any pets."

Greta rolled her eyes. "I know how you are. That's going to last about as long as your 'one dog at a time' rule. Remind me, how many dogs do you own?"

Tess glanced to make sure Belinda wasn't looking, then stuck her tongue out at her sister. She grabbed the movie from the pile on the dresser next to the television—Greta optimistically invested in other kids' movies on the off chance that Belinda would agree to watch something other than *Finding Nemo* sometime—then put the disk in the DVD player and handed the remote to Belinda.

"Which button?" she asked, studying the device.

"You've done this five hundred times, kid," Greta said.

"Which button?"

"The arrow," Tess said, pointing to it. Belinda pressed the button and handed the remote back to Tess, then snuggled closer to Greta.

"You know it's the arrow button," Greta told her.

"Yes," Belinda said tranquilly, eyes glued to the screen.

Tess took the dishes downstairs to the kitchen and loaded the dishwasher. She made sure Greta had rolls and juice for the morning, then took a moment to glance at the newspaper she'd brought in with the dinner. Feeling virtuously informed about what the city council was up to, she put the paper in the recycling bin, then remembered that Greta had a trash pickup the next morning and brought the trash can to the curb.

After she came back in, she called Greta's friend Monica to make sure she was still planning to stop in and help Greta get dressed before heading to work in the morning. The usual stab of guilt made her wince. She knew Monica should have her job—she'd wanted her job. But when Tess had screwed up again three years ago, blood had been thicker than friendship.

"You're my sister," Greta had said at the time, as if that meant the case was closed. Tess had almost wept with gratitude. After all, her parents had said, "You brought this on yourself. We can't help you." *Won't* help you, they meant. And in a way she knew they were exactly right; she had brought this on herself by taking in strays. But what if Greta had said that? Tess and Belinda had nothing. At the time, Tess had been looking for work for several months. They wouldn't have been able to pay the rent. She could have lost Belinda to foster care. Never, ever would she do a thing that could hurt Belinda. Never again.

Tess shook herself and walked back up the stairs. Just lucky that she had one person in her life willing to help out during the hard times.

"Greta's eyes are closed," Belinda reported when she spotted Tess in the doorway.

"I bet she's sleeping. She's had a tough day."

"Stayed on her good side."

"Very clever of you. Nemo's almost done, isn't he?"

"Have to swim down."

"Okay." Tess tidied the room, setting out clean

loungewear for Monica to help Greta put on in the morning, gathering discarded clothes and bundling them into the painted wicker hamper. She double-checked that Greta's phone was within easy reach, fretting for a moment about leaving her alone for the night. But Greta and the surgeon had agreed it was fine and Tess knew Greta would sleep better without being disturbed by Belinda's frequent night wakings.

Tess glanced at Greta's appointment book to see what time her physical therapy appointment was set for the following afternoon, and then *Nemo* was over and Belinda slid off the bed without arguing, and they left Greta peacefully sleeping in her soft cocoon of blankets and pillows.

Back at home, Tess fixed herself a quick sandwich, let Rufus (Labrador), Mooch (mutt of indeterminate origin), and Agnes (Irish setter) out for their last potty break before morning, rescued Penelope (Persian) from the top of the bookcase, cleaned up after the accident Max (elderly marmalade) had had, and put Rascal (hamster) back in his cage.

Then she got Belinda settled into bed, surrounded by her ever-changing array of stuffed animals and beginner books she couldn't read. Couldn't read *yet,* Tess reminded herself, and kissed Belinda on the forehead. Belinda eventually learned everything—hadn't she finally learned how to walk and how to talk? Now you couldn't get her to shut up. It just took her longer than it took other people and she wasn't always the best at the skill once she'd acquired it. But at least she learned.

"Good night, Belinda."

"Beautiful," Belinda reminded her.

"Good night, beautiful Belinda," Tess said.

"Forgot to tuck me in."

"I tucked you in."

"Forgot to kiss me."

"I kissed you."

"Forgot—"

"I love you, beautiful Belinda."

"Love you, beautiful Mama."

Tess smiled. Hearing that made every tough moment of the day disappear. Her daughter, like her sister, had a special kind of magic.

Chapter Two

Friday morning Tess faced the usual hectic scramble to get Belinda ready for school and herself ready for work, her efforts impeded and obstructed by the dogs and cats (not to mention the hamster, who escaped from his cage again). Tess sent Belinda to her bedroom to get her underwear on and ten minutes later when Tess checked, she found Belinda fishing train accessories out from under the desk.

"Focus, Belinda," she said, pulling a brush through her hair and wishing she'd packed Belinda's lunch the night before.

Belinda gave her a brilliant smile. "Focus!" she agreed.

Ten minutes later, she was hosting a tea party with the stuffed animals.

"We'll be late, Belinda," Tess warned. Belinda's face

31

crumpled in alarm because she hated being late to school. Not that this made her actually go any faster, Tess thought with a sigh, reminding herself to try setting the alarm another fifteen minutes earlier on Monday.

Belinda attended a small Montessori program run by an extremely gifted teacher whom Tess prayed would never retire, and with good-natured classmates whose parents Tess mostly liked. It was a supportive, nurturing environment and she knew Belinda was lucky to be in such a situation, but it came at a cost. Every month Tess sighed as she wrote the tuition check, then remembered Belinda's disastrous public school experiences and reminded herself that the tuition was cheap at the price. Certainly cheaper than a child who never reached her full potential or believed she was stupid because of the way those around her treated her.

Eventually everyone finished breakfast, including the animals, and Tess and Belinda ended up fully clothed and equipped. Tess grabbed the car keys and took Belinda's hand. Although school was only a few blocks away, they never seemed to have time to walk. Maybe Monday, Tess thought as they piled into the car.

In the school parking lot, she saw Jack—or was it Joe?—Ally's father (or perhaps stepfather). Ally's father and stepfather traded turns bringing her to school and Tess had never figured out who was who. Whoever it was, he waved at them and waited until they joined Ally and him on the sidewalk.

"Hi, Jack," Belinda said, swinging her lunchbox and jumping up the curb to the sidewalk. "Whatcha doing?"

"Hi, Belinda. I'm bringing Ally to school."

"Hi, Jack," Tess said on cue. Was Jack the one who was currently married to Ally's mom? And what was her name again?

"Where's Cheryl?" Belinda asked.

"She's at home, getting ready for work."

"Mama works," Belinda said proudly.

"That's good," Jack said, opening the door to the building and allowing them to precede him.

"Say hi to Cheryl for me," Tess put in. Thank goodness for Belinda's capacious memory for people's names and her unself-conscious inquisitiveness or Tess would never survive the social demands of dropping Belinda off at school.

"Here we are," she said as she pushed open the classroom door. She hugged Belinda, then watched her put her lunch box on the shelf and take a seat on the circle on the floor.

"Who is assistant today?" Belinda asked the teacher, Mrs. Phillips, not even sparing a glance for Tess. Smiling, Tess hurried back to her car, already focusing on what she needed to get done before school let out in the afternoon.

First thing, she stopped by Greta's house. Greta still looked tired and in pain but she seemed less pale than she had the previous night and the shadows under her eyes were not as pronounced. She was intently reading the morning paper but whipped off her glasses as soon as Tess came into the room.

"Hey, I know you wear bifocals," Tess said. "Everyone knows you wear bifocals."

"Not going down without a fight," Greta explained.

"Did you have breakfast?"

"Yes."

"Need anything?"

"Where's my laptop?"

"You're not doing any work until next week. It's Friday, enjoy your long weekend."

"I'm wracked with pain," Greta said, somewhat more overdramatic than usual. "I'm not expecting to enjoy myself very much. I might as well work."

"You can watch *Finding Nemo* again with Belinda tonight," Tess said, patting her on the shoulder. "That's something to look forward to."

Greta rolled her eyes. "At least hand me my appointment book. I need to call a few clients."

Tess did as she was asked, going to the desk to retrieve the leather-bound appointment book that Greta brought everywhere. She'd even tried to bring it to the hospital. Tess was convinced Greta would suffer from amnesia without the book, which detailed every aspect of her work and personal life. Not that Greta had any more of a personal life than Tess did. "Anything else?" Tess asked.

"Coffee."

"Yes'm. Skinny latte?"

"Make it a fat double mocha. I need my strength."

"You bet."

"Tess?"

"Yeah?"

"Thanks."

"That's what sisters are for."

"There you go," Greta said. "I knew you'd catch on eventually."

Kevin, the burly bearded barista, started the espresso the minute Tess walked in the door of La Prima Tazza. The small coffee shop was dim and quiet, the morning rush over and the lunch rush not yet started. Tess could hear the overhead fans squeaking in the tin ceiling as they stirred the warm air. Spring had come with a vengeance: It was already in the eighties and the Victorian-era building that housed the coffee shop didn't boast central air.

A few students hunched over laptops on the two long dining room–style tables—the building might not have air-conditioning but it did have wireless Internet access, which Tess knew was more important than refrigerated air to the students. A retired couple sat at one of the small marble-topped tables scattered around the space, arguing about the merits of a proposed ban on cell phone use while driving in the city. Apparently the male half of the couple thought he could win the argument merely by raising his voice.

"The usual?" Kevin asked as she stepped up to the

counter. His red hair had been cut extremely short in what looked like an accidental style—no one could really have meant to do that—so Tess didn't comment on it.

"For me. Greta wants a fat double mocha."

"Knee surgery, right? How'd it go?"

"She's a little snappish. When I left she was on the phone hassling vendors."

"Good thing she has you to smooth out the ruffled feathers afterward," Kevin said as he poured chocolate syrup into a small metal pitcher of milk. The comment was his idea of a joke. He knew Greta often had to deal with the consequences of what she called Tess' "direct-ness," the main reason Tess wasn't allowed to have much personal contact with the clients.

"Ha ha," Tess said sourly as Kevin slid the two Styro-foam cups toward her. She paid him for the coffee, tuck-ing her change in the tip jar. She resisted adding a biscotti or a muffin to her order. She fought the same bat-tle every day. The muffins were winning. "Look at me."

"Looking," Kevin said, leaning forward, his elbows on the counter.

"If you were unattached, what would you see?" Tess asked.

Kevin made a face. "No way. I'm not dumb enough to answer a question I can only get wrong."

"All right. Here's the deal. I met a guy. Straight and unattached, according to Greta. He didn't even flirt with me."

"And?" Kevin asked.

"Do I look like someone who objects to flirting?"

"Umm, yeah," Kevin said. "But nothing wrong with looking professional and businesslike when you're, you know, on business."

"Hmm."

"You just need to relax," Kevin advised her. "You look a little straight-laced in that shirt. It's like something Greta would wear. That's all I'm saying."

"I'm supposed to look like a professional."

"Try to work with me, Tess."

"I'll keep it in mind."

"And stop wearing your hair up like that. It's okay for Greta but you've got that flamboyant gypsy look going for you. You don't do subtle very well."

"Thanks," Tess said, feeling like she'd gotten a little more information than she'd bargained for. "When did you start your fashion consulting business?"

"Hey, I'm a guy. I know guys. Not all of us go for that Chanel Number Five thing Greta does."

" 'Not all' meaning 'no more than ninety-nine percent'?"

Kevin grinned. "Would it work better if I said he's obviously an idiot for not flirting with you?"

"Thank you," Tess said. "Exactly as I suspected."

"Got your coffee," Tess said to Greta, handing her one of the cups and setting the other down on the nightstand. "May I borrow your comb?"

"Sure. Why?" Greta took a sip of her coffee, her

gaze not moving from the notes she was making on her laptop. If Tess confiscated the laptop, Greta would find a legal pad and scribble on that instead. So much for taking the day off.

"Kevin says I shouldn't wear my hair up." Tess pulled the clip out of her hair and let her dark curls fall to her shoulders, then ran the comb through. She squinted at the result in the mirror above Greta's French provincial dresser. Just as she'd thought. Now she looked like she should be telling fortunes and reading palms. All that was missing was the peasant blouse and gold hoop earrings.

She could see her own dark eyes flashing with irritation at what she saw. It wouldn't be so bad if she actually had some psychic ability to go with the looks. Then she might be able to get out of the way of what was coming. Or at least see that it was on its way.

"He's right," Greta said, looking up from the laptop. "Who's Kevin?"

"Barista, La Prima Tazza."

"Do I know him?"

"You see him every day. Except weekends. And when you're laid up after getting your knee repaired."

"Wait. You're taking fashion advice from the man who makes our coffee?"

"He's a guy," Tess explained. "Knows what guys like. Obviously, trying to emulate your style isn't working for me."

"That would be because we're nothing alike. We don't look alike, we don't have similar personalities, we don't have the same taste in clothes. Or men."

"Hey, I like all kinds of men," Tess protested.

"Exactly," Greta responded.

Tess stuck her tongue out at Greta, which, though childish, was the only sensible response to Greta's teasing. Then she set the comb down and stuck her tongue out at her own reflection in the mirror.

"You may not have Prince Charming, but at least you have me," Greta said. The words brought a smile to Tess' lips.

"Fairy godmother."

"What?" Greta asked, startled.

"When I was a little kid, that's how I thought of you," Tess said, not admitting that it was how she still thought of her sister. "You used to swoop in and fix things. Like that time you used your money from your after-school job to buy me Pamela's old three-speed."

"It was twenty bucks. It was that or buy fashion magazines and I decided to be noble that weekend."

"See? Fairy godmother," Tess said lightly. "I get my disposition for fixing things from you."

"Don't blame that on me," Greta said, narrowing her eyes and wagging a finger at Tess. "Don't think I don't see exactly what you're doing. Look, Tess, it's sweet that you remember those things but I couldn't manage much. I couldn't take you away from it."

"It meant a lot at the time, Greta. Those little things were all I had. And even when you didn't win the fight, at least I knew you were on my side."

"I can't help it if you're my sister," Greta said.

"It's not just that," Tess said. "How many times have you disagreed with something I planned to do?"

"Approximately ten thousand seven hundred and forty-nine," Greta said. "Not that I'm counting."

"So what do you do?"

"When I disagree with you? I try to talk you out of it."

"And if you fail?'

Greta looked at her. "I always fail," she said. "So you should rephrase that question. *When* I fail, I usually take a yoga class to calm my nerves."

Tess shook her head. "And when you fail to talk me out of it, you hold my coat for me while I wade in there," she said. "And you pat me on the shoulder when I land on my behind, and you say, 'Atta girl.' You never say, 'I told you so.' "

"Look, Tess. You're the bravest person I know. When I try to dissuade you from a course of action, it's not because I think you're wrong. It's because I think you'll get hurt. I can't stand seeing you get hurt. It doesn't seem to bother you half as much as it bothers me. Of course I'm not going to say, 'I told you so.' Just having this conversation is giving me a headache."

"You're pretty amazing," Tess said. "You know that, right?"

Greta took a deep breath. "Don't you have work to do, kid?"

"I love you too," Tess said.

"Where's the fabric for the Dunkirk kitchen curtains?" Tess asked, standing in the doorway to Greta's bedroom, hands on hips. It was Monday morning and she was trying to organize the materials she needed for the next few days, a task that required Herculean efforts because, unlike Greta, Tess wasn't naturally efficient. "I've got everything else."

"Where'd you put it?" Greta asked, picking up the remote to mute the design show she was criticizing.

"You know, they can't hear you when you talk to them like that."

"You're the one who won't let me work," Greta said. "How else am I supposed to pass the time?"

"Read. Reflect. Meditate. Sleep."

"Boring," Greta said. She looked at Tess, her eyes widening as she did so. "What's this?"

"I give up," Tess said. Thin gold bracelets jangled as she pushed a cloud of dark hair off her face. Gold hoops in her ears caught the light as she moved. "I'm just going to go with it. I have been fighting it all my life and I'm tired of the battle."

"That blouse is going to give Mr. Dunkirk a heart attack."

"That's not my problem," Tess said.

"Uh-huh," said Greta. "You are a cruel, cruel woman."

"I'm embracing who I am," Tess said. "Grandma always said I was the gypsy of the family."

"Grandma would know," Greta said. "Have you tried your new look out on Kevin?"

"His jaw dropped," Tess admitted. "And he gave me two thumbs up."

"There you go then." With a wave of her hand, Greta dismissed that topic of conversation. "What else are you missing?" she asked, referring to the original topic.

"Just that cotton print for the Dunkirk kitchen. I put it in the storage closet when it arrived and now I can't find it."

"You looked carefully?"

"No, Greta. I'm just bugging you for fun. Of course I looked carefully."

"Let me think. That came last week, right?"

"Right."

"What else did we do last week?"

"You finished the Dupree townhouse and presented the final bill, which they meekly paid like good little lambs. You tried to sell the Gomezes on a redesign of their three-season room but they decided to go to Bermuda instead."

"Okay."

"You pitched the new law office downtown because you had the insane idea that companies would be easier to work with than individual clients."

"Meeting them quickly disabused me of that notion," Greta said.

"That was quite an indemnity clause they wanted you to sign."

"That reminds me. I moved the fabric to the trunk of my car because I wanted to show it to Geraldine Warder. I'm trying to convince her to put some cotton curtains in her kitchen but she had the idea that they would look cheap."

"At that price? I don't think so," Tess said. She found Greta's car keys on the dresser, then dashed downstairs and out the front door to transfer the parcel to her own car. Then she brought the keys back to Greta's bedroom and asked, "Anything else before I get started on those curtains?"

But Greta had curled up on the velvet pillows like an elegant cat and was sound asleep. Tess left a note for Greta to call her when she was ready for lunch, then slipped out to finish her morning tasks.

Tess was pinning up the hem of the Dunkirk curtains when she realized it was time to pick up Belinda from school. A quirk of tension started between her shoulder blades. She'd hoped to finish hemming the curtains before Belinda came home, but now it would have to wait until after the little girl went to bed, when Tess had planned to curl up with her sketchbook and maybe some of her special stash of good chocolate. Now working on her fabric designs was out. Not that she'd figured out what she'd do with her portfolio once she developed it. At the rate she was going, it didn't matter. She'd never get the portfolio done.

Everything always seemed to take slightly longer than it should so she was always running behind and adjusting her schedule on the fly. She envied relaxed and unhurried Michael the luxury of time he seemed to enjoy. But, she reminded herself, he didn't have a family. If she had to choose between having time and having Belinda, it was an easy choice to make.

She folded the fabric and gathered a few stray pins, then bundled everything into the modified walk-in closet that served as her sewing room. When she and Belinda had moved into this tiny rental duplex three years ago, Tess had felt clever and creative for converting the space, but now she wished she had more room for her work. It was impossible to carve out more here. Greta's small Victorian was already overrun with all the accoutrements of the business and she didn't have any spare place to set up a sewing room. Tess hated complaining about her cramped quarters because the only other option was to rent a space. Although Interiors was doing well, Greta wasn't making enough extra profit to rent an office or a workshop. Employing Tess full-time already stretched her resources. Tess knew Greta would have done better with a part-timer to help with the administrative tasks and subcontracting the sewing out to a seamstress, but that hadn't stopped Greta from giving Tess the full-time job when she'd needed it.

And while the salary was fair, it was by no means

luxurious. Between rent and tuition and insurance and groceries and utilities and all the other expenses of being a single mother with a grade-schooler, there was never much money left over at the end of the month. So moving into bigger digs herself wasn't feasible at the moment. Besides, a bigger rental place wasn't what she wanted. What she wanted . . . she couldn't discuss with Greta. Even contemplating the conversation made her feel ungrateful. *Working for you is not enough,* she'd have to say, and that sounded greedy.

It didn't matter, anyway. Tess had a good life, better than she had once imagined it could be. *Be grateful for what you have,* Tess reminded herself. *It took you a long time to get this much.*

Chapter Three

"Here or to go?" Kevin asked when Tess came into the coffee shop later in the week on a warm Wednesday morning.

"Here," Tess said firmly. She was entitled to take a few minutes for herself, even though it was a workday. She worked plenty of evenings and weekends, especially when Greta bit off more than she could chew, which happened more frequently than not as she tried to make her business evermore successful. Even as Tess formed the thought, she shook her head. Greta would never ask Tess to account for her time that way. Tess was a lot harder on herself than her boss was.

She took the coffee over to one of the small marble-topped tables by the window where she could see passersby strolling down Massachusetts Street, then dug her sketchpad and colored pencils out of her bag and started sketching. As the pencil moved, she smiled. Another of her crazy fantasies, she thought as the design took shape. At art school, she had always been most interested in applied arts, which was how and why she'd learned to sew. She'd loved textiles and what you could do with them. Unfortunately, art fabric installations didn't pay the bills. But unlike some of the other artists she'd gone to school with, at least she'd learned a useful, if retro, skill. Which was not to say she'd ever imagined making her living sewing things. While it wasn't always artistic, she enjoyed the craft, working with fabric, seeing the yardage take shape and become something useful.

With a twinge, she thought of Michael and his furniture. She'd bet he felt the same way about wood. Taking the raw unfinished piece and turning it into something beautiful and functional. Her mind drifted to the hard planes of his face and the slow smile that made him seem so appealing, the muscles bulging under his T-shirt as he moved, the narrow hips as he sauntered down the hallway. . . . She shook herself. *Focus, Tess,* she told herself firmly. She was here to work.

A few minutes later, she leaned back and looked at the colors on the page. She should tell Greta about what she wanted to do. Greta would probably have suggestions. Greta always did. But Tess didn't want to owe

Greta anything else. She wanted this to be hers, really hers. Still, it was hard to see how she could make her dream come true.

She slipped the sketchbook in her purse. Maybe it was time to let go of the dream.

"Michael's got a problem," Greta said when Tess stopped by her house that afternoon. Though still mostly confined to the bedroom, Greta could maneuver around on her crutches and was trying to catch up on the work she'd missed during her immediate post surgery recuperation. Unfortunately, since she wasn't able to do site visits right now, her ability to make up for lost time was limited.

At the moment, she was sitting on her bed, fat pillows propping her injured leg up as she put a proposal together, assembling sketches and fabric swatches into a presentation folder. That was usually Tess' job because she had an eye for arranging the sketches and swatches in an appealing, readable way, but Greta apparently felt the need for busywork since she couldn't do much else at the moment. Anything to assuage the restlessness, Tess assumed.

"Let me guess," Tess said, handing Greta the mail she'd collected from the box. "Michael's problem has become your problem."

"Not my problem," Greta clarified. "Yours. His upholsterer is overbooked and can't do a project as promised. Michael was hoping you could lend a hand and do the cushion for that settee he's making for the Weatherhills."

"I'm not an upholsterer," Tess said. Not that she objected to helping Michael. On the contrary, she was ready, willing, and able. Just thinking about Michael's slow, gentle smile made her heart thud and her palms sweat. However, she knew she should stay away from him. He wasn't interested and she couldn't fix him. She knew that in her brain. Unfortunately, her brain didn't seem to be in charge.

"It's just a cushion," Greta said, dismissing Tess' objection with a wave of her hand, tossing the mail on the nightstand. Tess knew that was just for show. Nothing interested Greta more than checking the mail for money. "Same as a pillow, and you do those for me all the time. Michael's got the materials and specs for you." She spoke as if the deal had already been agreed to. And why not? It wasn't as if Michael had asked Tess out on a date. He just wanted her to sew something. That was what she did for a living. It was strictly business.

The realization discouraged her. *After we met, he thought of me. He thought of me to do his sewing.*

"Yes, but—" Tess wasn't quite sure how to put her main objection to the plan. *Didn't you warn me?* she wanted to ask. *Didn't you tell me I couldn't fix him? So here I am, trying to not fix him and you're forcing me to spend time with him? What's with that?*

"He's going to pay you for a rush job," Greta said, using the coaxing tone of voice that Tess remembered very well from their youth. "It'd go a long way toward a vacation for you and Belle." Ah, now she was bringing in the big guns.

"It'll mean putting off the drapes for that model home," Tess said as a test. Greta always set her priorities and never changed them on a whim. The model home drapes were a priority.

"The builder's behind schedule anyway."

Okay, the model home drapes *had been* a priority. What was Greta up to? Tess thought about asking her sister but decided she'd never get a straight answer. "Doesn't that contractor ever hit a deadline?" she asked, highly suspicious. "If you never finished a project on time, wouldn't you step back and evaluate why that might be so?"

"It's construction, kid," Greta said. "They'd have a heart attack if you suggested they were actually supposed to adhere to their deadlines."

"Doesn't it drive you nuts? You have to meet your deadlines even if they're late getting the windows in or the room turns out to be different dimensions from the ones listed on the blueprints."

"They pay me to work my magic," Greta said. "You know that. You've been at it long enough. What's bothering you?"

"Just whining. Belinda was a pain this morning. All I do is work and take care of her. I have no life." *I meet attractive men and they want me to sew things for them.*

"You've always seemed perfectly happy doing what you're doing."

"I am happy," Tess said. "Just, you know . . ."

"You have no life," Greta said.

"Exactly."

"So what are you going to do about it?"

"Not a single thing," Tess said and grinned.

"As long as you have a plan," Greta said.

Tess glanced at the dashboard clock in her beat-up Ford Escort. She would just have time to pick up the fabric and specs from Michael before collecting Belinda from school. Assuming this light ever turned green, she thought, tapping her fingers on the steering wheel.

A few minutes later, she parked in the now-familiar gravel lot and walked into the metal building. This time the showroom assistant was seated at the front desk and she smiled warmly when Tess walked in. The assistant was an older, slightly plump gray-haired woman wearing discreet makeup and a neatly tailored pantsuit that made Tess feel sweaty and rumpled next to her. The assistant—Renee, according to the nameplate on a corner of the desk—picked up the phone on the desk and punched in an extension after Tess stated her business. She spoke briefly, then hung up the phone and gave Tess another smile.

"Michael's in the workshop. He said to go right back."

"I just need the fabric and specs," Tess said, knowing

that her resistance to spending time with Michael wasn't only because she was afraid of being late to pick up Belinda.

"He wants you to see the settee," Renee explained.

Tess refrained from rolling her eyes. Greta had emphasized that you couldn't express your feelings in front of the client—or the client's employees—and Michael was a client now. But why was he wasting her time? It was a settee. She knew what a settee looked like. With a sigh, she reminded herself that he was paying her way more than the job was worth. She could indulge him.

"Down the main aisle, turn right at the bathroom sink, then through the double doors," Renee said with a smile, pointing toward the main aisle.

Tess didn't need the directions but she thanked the assistant for them anyway, then made her way to the workshop. Pushing open the door, she spotted Michael right away. He was leaning over the settee, sanding the seat by hand, using a soft cloth to wipe away the dust. The sight of him made her stomach turn over. Why did she have to react to him this way? Wasn't life complicated enough without being interested in a man who didn't return the favor? A man who, when he thought of her, thought, *good with a needle*?

Dimly she was aware that his assistant—Jimmy?—was moving around the shop, but she didn't spare him a glance. All of her attention was riveted on the man in front of her. He seemed so completely involved in his work that she almost hated to disturb him. On the other hand, he was the one who'd commanded her presence.

"Looks beautiful," she said, not specifying what she thought was beautiful.

He looked up, startled, then gave a slow smile. Yes, there went her heart, thudding frantically at the gentle, lazy smile, given just for her. His brown eyes still had the sad look. If he were a cocker spaniel, she could just take him home, introduce him to Rufus, Mooch, and Agnes, and be done with it. But he wasn't. No, he had to be a *man*. The last man with sad eyes had stolen her money and stomped on her heart. She was still pretty upset about the money.

"I'm proud of this piece," he said, running a hand along the back of the settee.

"Greta said you just want a bench cushion." *Remember what you came for,* Tess told herself. It wasn't to set herself up for another broken heart. It wasn't to bring home another stray.

"Yeah," Michael said. "The client wants to leave the seat back exposed."

"I can see why. It's beautiful."

He smiled again, then raised his voice and called, "Jimmy!" The assistant looked up from the rack of wood he was perusing. "Where's the Weatherhill stuff?" Michael asked, setting the sandpaper and cloth down.

Jimmy dusted his hands off, walked over to the metal shelves and pulled a package down. Then he ducked into the office and reappeared with a folder. He brought the package and folder to Michael without saying anything.

"Fabric and specs," Michael announced, handing them over to Tess.

"If you don't mind"—*and even if you do*, she didn't say, having learned from Greta—"I'll double-check the measurements." Tess pulled a tape measure from her bag as she spoke, then leafed through her sketchbook to find a blank page where she could record her notes.

"How thick do you want the cushion?" she asked, crouching to measure the seat width.

"I have the foam here," Michael said, gesturing toward a rack. Tess followed the movement, saw the foam slotted into the rack. Jimmy stood, hands on hips, looking at sheets of plywood but not moving. Tess had the feeling he was listening to every word she and Michael said. She didn't know why. Their conversation wasn't very interesting. She wasn't saying anything she wanted to say.

"That foam is not going to fit in my car," she said. "I'll have to pick it up later." Greta had an old box truck they used for just such purposes.

"That's fine." Then after a brief hesitation, Michael asked, "What are those sketches?" He pointed at her sketchbook.

"Oh." She suddenly felt flustered though she wasn't exactly sure why. "Just some ideas I had." She flipped the sketchbook closed.

"May I see?" he asked, holding out a hand. Apparently he wasn't a subtle man and didn't understand what it meant when she'd flipped the book closed. She glared at him. His smile dimmed, a little uncertain. Oh, that wasn't fair. He was using underhanded tactics now, making her think the smile might disappear if she didn't cooperate.

"Sure," she said, reluctantly surrendering the book to him. His smile deepened as he took the book.

Michael turned back to the first page, then leafed slowly through the book. Tess couldn't tell what he was thinking from his expression but she knew she was holding her breath and that knowledge only further irritated her.

Jimmy was frankly staring at them now, eyes narrowed. Tess flinched away from his gaze. He knew what Tess wanted from Michael, and it wasn't a kitchen cabinet.

"These are fabric designs?" Michael asked without looking up from the book.

"Yes."

"You have a whimsical imagination."

"Yes," she said, and couldn't help feeling disappointed. Was that all he had to say? She had a whimsical imagination? She bit down on the almost overwhelming desire to snatch the book back from him.

"This is my favorite," he said, finally looking up and giving her the slow smile again as he tapped a page. The smile made it hard to breathe. A woman could get used to that smile. That was an addictive smile. Better than chocolate. A woman wouldn't need chocolate if she could get that smile on a regular basis.

Stop it, Tess told herself sternly. Why did she care

what some carpenter she didn't even know thought about her drawings—or about her?

She looked at the page he indicated and broke into a grin. "That's my favorite too," she said, touching one of the dragons. Red and gold and green, they cavorted on a background sky of light blue, playing cards, reading books, blowing bubbles, playing instruments, doing the backstroke in the clouds.

"These are really good. Your more traditional designs are attractive but the whimsical ones are best." She noticed he didn't preface any of his comments with "I think" or "in my opinion." She wished she could have that confidence, that assurance. Or possibly it was arrogance.

"Thanks," she said, holding her hand out for the book. He didn't give it back to her right away. Not a subtle man, she reminded herself. She'd probably have to kick him in the shin to get it away from him.

"Have you thought about doing anything with your designs? What does Greta say?"

"Greta doesn't know."

Michael raised a brow. "Why not?"

"I don't want to owe her more than I already do," Tess said, then wished she could bite back the words. Why was she talking about this difficult subject with a man she barely knew?

"What does that mean?"

Tess sighed. "Whenever I screw up, which is more than you might expect, Greta picks me up and dusts me off." She hoped the explanation said enough. Greta might say Tess was brave, but mostly her mistakes seemed stupid and incompetent, not courageous.

Michael regarded her. "It doesn't sound that way when she talks about you."

Tess hunched a shoulder. "That's what it feels like," she said, hating how defensive she felt. "Anyway, fabric design is a tiny, highly competitive field. I'd have to move to New York and apprentice for years to have a shot at designing for real."

He finally handed over the book, which she snatched from his fingers and tucked safely away in her handbag. "And you can't do that because . . . ?" he asked.

"Because I'm not twenty anymore. Because I can't just move to New York and live with five roommates in a studio apartment for ten years while I claw my way up from slave wages. Because I have a daughter with problems and I finally found a good school for her. And it probably sounds like excuses to you, but I'm just too tired to try." Tess closed her eyes. That was the story she told herself when she grew frustrated at not being able to do the work she loved for a living but she didn't know if the story was true.

Michael didn't say anything right away, and she almost hoped he wouldn't say anything at all. After a moment, he said slowly, as if choosing his words carefully, "They're good designs. Maybe moving to New York isn't the only way." It wasn't exactly a challenge to the story she told, but she didn't dare explore it further. She didn't want to find out what he meant. She knew by now how dangerous it was to have dreams. The sensible thing was to keep your head down and do your work.

"Maybe. I'll get this done in the next day or two," Tess said, indicating the settee and changing the subject. "I'll be back this afternoon to pick up the foam."

She grabbed the materials Michael had given her and made her escape.

Michael sighed as the double doors of the workshop closed after Theresa's swaying hips. She'd caught him by surprise again. She was a talented designer but she seemed to have given up on her dream. Circumstances, he knew, could make even modest dreams seem impossibly out of grasp. Hadn't he experienced that himself?

That moment of vulnerability when she'd talked about her dreams had touched him. Sure, he'd been attracted to her. He'd have to be blind not to be. But did he also have to start liking her? Wanting to help her? What was wrong with him? He had no interest in starting anything with anyone. His life was just fine the way it was. It was *perfect.*

What was important was for him to focus on building his business and staying as far away from romantic entanglements as he could get. Even as he thought it, he was looking forward to seeing her again. Shaking his head, he turned back to the settee and realized Jimmy was staring at him.

"What?" he asked.

"What happened to Peterson?"

"Nothing happened to Peterson."

"Then why are you giving an upholstery job to that girl?" Jimmy asked suspiciously.

Well, if Michael was going to lie about things—"my upholsterer is overbooked"—he needed to be better at it. He shrugged elaborately, picking up the sandpaper and cloth. "She comes highly recommended. I just thought I'd give her a trial run in case I ever need a backup."

"Uh-huh," Jimmy said. "A man often needs a backup *upholsterer.* For chrissake, Michael."

"Don't you have work to do?"

"Dial 9-1-1," Jimmy said. "We've got an upholstery emergency!"

"Shut up, Jimmy."

"Doctor, get this man an upholsterer! Stat!"

"Do you like your job, Jimmy? Because if you don't shut up, you're fired."

Tess picked up Belinda from school, then drove to Greta's house to get the truck so she could pick up the foam from Michael's shop. She left her little Ford at the curb, then strapped Belinda into the truck and gave her the standard pep talk.

"When we get there, say hello to Mr. Manning," she told Belinda.

"Okay."

"And if he asks, 'How are you?' what do you say?"

"Good," Belinda answered promptly. Tess thought

about correcting the "good" to "fine" but decided not to fight more than the necessary battles. A simple correction like that could easily lead to a ten-minute distraction and cause Belinda to lose track of the important parts of the conversation.

"Don't touch anything."

"Is that the rule?"

"That's the rule."

"When is dinner?"

"When is dinner?" Tess said. "We have dinner at the same time every single night of our lives."

"When is dinner?" Belinda repeated.

"Six o'clock," Tess said, starting the truck. Greta wouldn't have given the answer so quickly. But Greta didn't deal with Belinda all day and all night and she wasn't Belinda's mother. Plus Greta was significantly more stubborn than even Belinda was.

"McDonald's?"

"No."

"Why?"

"We're fixing dinner for Greta."

"Why?"

"It's healthier. McDonald's is a treat. We only do it now and then."

"But why?"

"Because I said so," Tess said and flashed a grin.

"McDonald's is good," Belinda said, trying another tack.

"Belinda, honey, Mommy already said no," Tess said.

"Don't like no."

"Nobody likes no," she said, thinking of Michael. He was certainly saying it loud and clear. "But that's the answer sometimes."

"Where are we going?"

"I just told you."

"Pick up foam."

"That's right."

"What's foam?"

"You know what foam is."

"Do not."

"The soft stuff inside cushions and pillows," Tess said.

"Pillows!" Belinda grinned.

"Yep."

"Pillows are soft."

"Yep."

"Where are we going?"

Patience, Tess reminded herself. Being Belinda's mother was definitely about learning patience.

"I love you, Belinda," she said out loud. That was always good for distracting Belinda.

"Love *you,* Mommy," Belinda said.

"Do you know how much I love you?" Tess asked. "This much!"

"This much!" Belinda echoed, stretching her arms out wide.

"We're here," Tess said a few minutes later, pulling into the parking lot outside Michael's shop and shutting off the truck. She twisted in her seat to look at Belinda. "Do you remember the rules?"

"Say hello, good, don't touch," Belinda recited.

"That's it," Tess said. "Here we go."

She climbed out, helped Belinda down and ushered her into the building. No showroom assistant sat at the front desk, so she led the way directly to the double doors in back, Belinda sauntering along behind her, staring at the furniture. Tess paused for Belinda to catch up with her. *We're on Belinda time now,* she reminded herself and swallowed an impatient, "Come on!"

"Bedroom, Mama," Belinda said, staring at the furniture grouping in front of her.

"Sure is. You know how Mama said Mr. Manning makes furniture? That's some of the furniture he makes."

"Don't touch," Belinda said, her fingers inching forward as if of their own volition.

"That's right," Tess said, capturing Belinda's hand in hers. She understood the temptation to run her fingers along the glossy smooth surfaces.

Belinda pulled her hand free, giving Tess a glare. "Big girl," she said.

"All right," Tess said, surrendering. Belinda clenched her hands into fists and didn't touch anything. Tess pushed open the double doors to the workshop, didn't see anything immediately dangerous to young children, like circular saws in operation, and beckoned Belinda in behind her. The workshop was silent—and deserted. She glanced around. Should she just take the foam and leave a note? Much as she was tempted—he wanted her for her *sewing skills*?—she knew she should let Michael know she was there.

She went to the door on the left, which stood partially open. She knocked and peered around the frame. As she'd thought, the door led to an office. Built-in cabinets lined two walls, and file cabinets marched along a third. Michael sat at the desk in the center of the room with his back to the door, staring at a handful of papers. He rubbed his neck as she watched. Papers, file folders, sticky notes and empty Styrofoam coffee cups that she recognized as coming from La Prima Tazza littered the desk.

"Hey, Michael," she said.

He glanced up with a start. "Sorry, I didn't hear you come in," he said. "The buzzer back here is supposed to go off when someone comes in the front door." He indicated a small sound box set in the wall.

Tess opened her mouth to make a suggestion, then closed it. It wasn't her problem. She didn't need to fix it. "We're here for the foam," she said. "My daughter, Belinda, is with me."

At the sound of her name, Belinda stuck her head around the corner, her eyes bright with excitement, a smile curving her lips. She always liked meeting new people and as a consequence they usually liked meeting her.

"This is Belinda," Tess said. "Say hello to Mr. Manning."

"Hello, Mr. Manning," Belinda said. She marched over to the desk and planted herself in front of it.

Michael grinned and came around the desk to crouch near her. He seemed to instinctively understand that she responded more like a younger child. "Hello, Belinda."

"Belle," Belinda said.

"Oh, okay." Michael slanted a glance at Tess. Well, hadn't he heard of people having nicknames before? "Hello, Belle. How old are you?"

"Good," Belinda said promptly.

Michael slanted another glance at Tess, who said gently, "How old are you, Belinda? That's what Mr. Manning asked."

"Eight years old," Belinda said.

"Eight," Michael said. A shadow crossed his face and his smile faltered. "Eight. That's a good age."

Belinda looked up at Tess. Tess knew she wasn't sure how to respond since the comment hadn't been part of their plan. "The best," Tess prompted.

"The best," Belinda echoed.

"I'm glad to meet you," Michael said. Belinda nodded, with another reproachful glance at Tess for not having coached her with an appropriate response to that. Until she knew a person better, interactions were far easier for Belinda if she'd practiced a script first, but that approach obviously had its drawbacks.

"Let's get that foam," Michael said to Tess. "I'll help you haul it out to the truck."

Tess turned to Belinda. "Can you sit right here?" She

pointed to the guest chair on the other side of Michael's desk. "We'll be just a minute. Here's some paper and a pencil. Draw me a picture, okay?"

Belinda accepted a few sheets of paper from Tess' sketchbook and a colored pencil from her bag.

"Red," she said, handing the blue pencil back to Tess. Tess dug in her bag and found a red pencil.

"Going to be an English teacher, I see," Michael said.

"What?" Belinda asked.

"Mr. Manning is teasing," Tess explained. "English teachers like red pencils."

Belinda's face broke into a grin. "Be a teacher!"

Tess gave her another smile and ruffled her hair again. "Don't touch anything."

"Okay," Belinda said, already bent over the paper, absorbed in her task. The pose reminded Tess briefly of Michael working on the settee.

She followed him out of the office and into the workshop. He pulled the foam from its slot on one of the racks and she caught one end while he took the other. They carried the foam out to Greta's box truck, wrestled it inside, then slammed the rear doors on it.

"Going to need any help getting it into your house?" Michael asked as they walked back to the workshop.

"I'll just put it on a sheet and drag it in that way," Tess said. "It's not heavy, just awkward. The sheet will protect it from any dirt." She had a lot of experience figuring out how to do things by herself. She had the sense that Michael did too.

"Thanks," Tess said. "I think that's everything. I'll just go grab Belinda and we'll get out of your hair."

When they returned to the office, Belinda was on the floor, her back turned toward them, playing with an object Tess couldn't see.

"What's that?" Tess asked, pushing the door all the way open and hoping it was something unbreakable, like a pen that had fallen to the floor.

"Look!" Belinda said excitedly, holding up a small carved wooden figure. "A giraffe. Two giraffes!" She clutched the second in her other hand. Moving into the office, Tess could see a veritable zoo of animals scattered across the floor.

"Where did you—" Tess noticed one of the cabinet doors ajar. She glanced over her shoulder at Michael, who stood still and motionless in the doorway, looking about as happy and expressive as the Sphinx.

Uh-oh, she thought.

"Mama asked you not to touch," Tess said gently, turning back to her daughter. Belinda froze. Then she scrambled to her feet, abandoning the animals on the floor. "Is Mama mad? Is Mama mad? Happy or mad?"

"Honey, I asked you not to touch—"

Belinda burst into tears. Tess knew Belinda became overly distraught if she thought her mother disapproved of something she'd done. Tess squatted and rubbed Belinda's back to reassure her.

"Sweetie, let's pick it up," she said. "That's all we

have to do to fix the problem." *I think.* She stroked Belinda's arm. She wanted to hug the little girl, but she was stiff and resistant. "Belinda, listen to Mama," Tess tried again, putting her cheek against Belinda's and trying to soothe her upset. "Calm down, sweetie. Mama is not mad. Mama asked you not to touch but you did. Now we have to pick everything up."

Belinda buried her face against Tess' shoulder. "Mama's not mad?"

"Mama's not mad," Tess said. "Come on, help me with this."

Belinda knelt down to pick up the animals, scrubbing the tears from her face. She handed over the giraffes. Tess moved to the cabinet to put them away. On the shelf, she saw a child-size Noah's Ark carved of sleek wood and painted bright, cheerful colors. "Oh, that's beautiful," she said. No wonder Belinda couldn't resist touching. Tess looked at the giraffes in her hands. They had purple spots and exaggerated, curving necks. She placed them on the shelf next to the ark. The zebra Belinda handed her next had pink and orange stripes and a goofy cross-eyed expression. Whimsical. Nothing at all like the man standing rigid and unspeaking in the doorway.

Tess put the last animal away and shut the cabinet door. She glanced around the office to make sure nothing had been overlooked. Then she bent down to Belinda and said, "I want you to say you're sorry to Mr.

Manning. You touched his things without permission. He's not mad"—*I hope*—"but you need to apologize for touching."

Belinda's lower lip trembled. She looked over Tess' shoulder at Michael. "Sorry," she whispered, before burying her face in Tess' neck.

Michael glanced down at her. "It's okay," he said. "No harm done."

"Sorry," Tess added, standing up and turning to face him, keeping a calming hand on Belinda's shoulder. "She's usually pretty good about listening to me."

"No problem," Michael said.

"It's really beautiful," Tess ventured. "You could sell—"

"I'd rather not talk about it," Michael said, and although his voice was calm and controlled, Tess could tell he was upset.

"Okay. We'd better go. I'll bring the finished cushion by as soon as I can." She took Belinda's hand and left the shop.

After they'd gone, Michael opened the cabinet and looked at the Noah's Ark and the animals inside. He touched the ark, remembering the hope he'd felt making it, the joy. He'd chosen the colors so it would look like a rainbow.

He hadn't meant to make Belinda and Theresa feel bad. It was just the shock of seeing a child play with the toy. How often had he imagined that? All the time he was carving the pieces, sanding them smooth, gluing them together, smiling as he painted the animals all those garish colors. His big hands had dwarfed the pieces but he'd imagined them just the right size in a child's small hands. *His* child's hands.

Belinda had been so absorbed in the animals, playing with them as he'd planned for that other child to do. When he saw the toy in her hands, it was like a kick in his gut. Seeing her with it brought back the old pain, the wound as ugly as ever. He wondered if the wound would ever heal. He'd gotten on with his life, but that wasn't the same thing. He touched the giraffe, then closed the cabinet door.

He wasn't ready for this. He leaned against the cabinet, head bent, his hands in his pockets. He wasn't ever going to be ready for this. He understood what Theresa wanted, what she was offering, but making a family out of what was left of their hearts, that was never going to happen. It was not in the cards. No matter what the gypsy thought she saw when she looked.

Chapter Four

The following Monday, Tess got up early and finished the cushion for Michael. She dropped Belinda off at school and picked up the truck from Greta's, then hauled the cushion to the truck and wrestled it into the back, thankful that the weather had held and that she didn't have to try to transport it during one of the many spring thunderstorms that often occurred this time of year.

Shutting the rear doors to the truck, she realized she hadn't made her La Prima Tazza run yet. She decided to bring a cup of coffee as a peace offering to Michael. It was the type of preemptive strike she'd used fairly successfully in the past with Greta. Now she hoped it would work on Michael. She didn't know what had upset him about Belinda's playing with the toy ark, but it couldn't hurt to talk about it over a cup of coffee.

Fortunately, it was still early enough in the morning for her to snag a parking space on Massachusetts Street, not far from the coffee shop. She dropped a dime in the meter and pushed open the glass door to the building. The rich smell of ground coffee beans immediately made her feel at home. She nodded at a couple of the other regulars as they patiently stood in line. Great. Her social life consisted of people she stood in line with. *Whose fault is that?* she chastised herself.

"What does Michael Manning drink?" she asked Kevin when it was her turn to be served.

"Michael Manning?" Kevin asked, scratching his beard. He prided himself on knowing what all the regulars drank, but she knew he found it easier to connect faces instead of names to the drinks.

"Carpenter, tall and rangy, brown eyes, light brown hair." If she said, *Cute smile, biceps that make a woman's heart skip a beat,* would she give herself away?

"Oh, yeah. He's a fan of Colombia's legal cash crop," Kevin said.

"You mean he takes regular coffee? That's it?"

"Yep."

"Not even a shot of vanilla?" Tess tried to fathom what kind of person would drink regular coffee when there was an entire menu of offerings just ready to pique the tongue while revving the metabolism. "I guess it can't be helped. Regular coffee for him, the usual for me. To go."

Kevin nodded and handed her a Styrofoam cup. She poured Colombian from one of the pots on the self-service counter as he fixed espresso for her drink.

"Sugar or milk?" she asked hopefully.

"Pretty sure he takes it straight."

Of course. Not a man who indulged himself. She shrugged and put a lid on the cup. He probably had no problem turning down muffins, either.

Kevin slid the cup of mocha across the counter and she handed him some cash. He stashed it in the till, then leaned toward her, lifting an eyebrow. "So what's up with Michael? Bringing him coffee? That's gotta mean something."

"You are such a gossip," Tess said. "Nothing is going on with Michael. I'm doing some work for him. That's all."

"Uh-huh," said Kevin, clearly not buying it. "I told you to wear your hair down, didn't I? I was right, wasn't I?"

"Yeah. That explains everything," she said and made a hasty exit.

What was it with her and making hasty exits lately? Tess wondered, groping on the seat next to her for her sunglasses. She seemed to be leaving a lot of places in a hurry. Her usual style was to confront whatever the problem was, spend a lot of energy battling it, beat her head against the wall for a while, then sink into an exhausted sleep. Fat lot of good that did her. Maybe she was just trying something new. Flight rather than fight. It seemed to work for other people. Why not her.

She shook her head as she pulled into the parking lot in front of Michael's shop. She climbed out of the truck, holding a coffee cup in each hand, shutting the door with her foot. She could almost hear Greta's protest as she did so: "Do you know why they call it a handle? Because you use your hand!"

She glanced over at the metal building. Yeah, look at her, running from trouble. See Tess flee. She took a deep, steadying breath. Two weeks ago, she'd had no idea about the wonders that building contained. Oh, innocence. Why couldn't she just forget things that weren't good for her? Why couldn't Greta have sent Michael the specs and samples by mail? Courier, if it came to that?

Tess pushed her way into the building and stopped when she saw the woman seated at the front desk. What was her name? She glanced surreptitiously at the nameplate. Renee. That was it. Too bad she couldn't bring Belinda with her to do the remembering of names.

"Hi, Renee," she said. "I have that cushion for Michael." She looked down at the two cups of coffee in her hand. "I stopped for coffee and thought I'd bring some by. Would you like a cup?" She hoped not because then there'd be none for her. But Greta made her be polite to the clients and their employees and/or families.

Renee shook her head. "No thanks, dear. I have to

avoid caffeine. Michael's in the back. Go on through. I'll let him know you're here."

"Thanks."

Tess strolled through the showroom, a little anxious about facing him. He'd seemed so upset the previous night. Still, what was he going to do, for heaven's sake? Fire her? If he was a jerk, she never had to speak to him again. Greta could handle him.

Admit it, Tess, she thought. He wasn't going to be a jerk. She was just anxious for other reasons. She pushed through the double doors and headed for the back office. She tapped the door with her elbow, heard his husky voice invite her in. The sound sent a skitter of pleasure along her nerve endings. Great. She was sensitized to the sound of his voice. She stepped inside the office and handed him one of the cups of coffee. He took it awkwardly, as if he wasn't sure why she was handing it to him.

"That's for you," she explained. Didn't anyone ever bring him things? "I was at La Prima Tazza, getting a coffee for me and thought you might like one too." She gestured at the Styrofoam cups littering his work surface. "I could tell you were a Tazza fan."

He laughed. "I guess it's pretty obvious," he said, sweeping a few of the old cups into the trash.

The sound of his laughter was deep and masculine, warm and smooth. The laughter eased away the drawn lines on his face. She took a breath and steadied herself.

You know, she told herself, *those women who propose*

marriage to serial killers on death row start by thinking they can fix things. They believed all it took was the love of a good woman. They were insane but they didn't start out that way. They probably started out normal, like anyone else, and then they took in their first stray. And before they knew it, they were writing love letters to murderers. *Love letters to murderers, Tess. Remember that.*

"Thank you," Michael said, rewarding her with that slow smile. An answering smile came to her lips. She couldn't help it. He took a sip of the coffee, then gave her a glance of surprise. "What is this?"

Tess swallowed a mouthful of plain black coffee from the cup in her hand, doing her best not to grimace. Great. She couldn't even get a peace offering right. "That'd be a mocha. Hot chocolate and espresso."

"Mmm," he said, taking another swallow. "Never had that before. It's really good."

"I have Colombian here, if you'd rather," Tess said, extending her cup. *Please trade.*

"No, this is fine. I like this."

Apparently he wasn't going to trade with her. She took another brave sip of the Colombian and swallowed it without gagging. It was fine. It would be better with chocolate or steamed milk or a dash of vanilla, but it was fine. Really.

She took a moment to regroup. What was she there for? Right. "Michael, I want to apologize for Belinda yesterday. She doesn't always remember everything I tell her. She tries really hard to be a good kid—"

Michael glanced at her in surprise. "No need to apologize," he said. "She seems like a real sweetheart."

"She is!" Tess said in a rush. "She just—you know, doesn't act like an eight-year-old. She has some—well, some problems. She manages really well, considering. But sometimes people don't understand."

"She was fine. Kids are curious. No problem."

"You seemed upset," Tess ventured. "She can tell that, you know? That's why she was crying. She was afraid we were really mad at her."

"Do people get mad at her a lot?" Michael asked.

"Not anymore," Tess said shortly. Then she took a deep breath and said, "My ex never adjusted, you know? He had these unreasonable expectations of her behavior and when she couldn't meet them . . ." She shrugged. "He took it out on her, even though she couldn't do more than she could do."

Michael nodded. "That sounds unhappy for everyone."

There was a lot of unnecessary unhappiness going around, she thought. It didn't have to be like that. Not if people were a little kinder, not so quick to judge or to blame. Sure. And when she was done organizing that, she'd get to work on war, crime, and poverty.

"Right," she said. "So even though he's been gone a long time, Belinda gets agitated if she thinks she's done something wrong, something that will make me or another grown-up mad at her."

"I'm sorry I upset her," Michael said. "It was just— I put that toy away a long time ago and I'd forgotten it

was there. Seeing it brought back some difficult memo-
ries."

"It's beautiful," Tess said. "I assume you made it?"

"I made it for my son."

Tess nodded but didn't say anything. She took another swallow of black coffee to keep her mouth occu-
pied. If nothing bad had happened, Michael wouldn't
have responded the way he had. She knew. She knew
how things didn't go the way you planned, the way they
were supposed to, the way they seemed to go for everyone else. Some people got to live the fairy tale, instead
of only pretending it could come true. He hadn't gotten
the fairy tale, either.

Don't say it, she thought, looking into his sad brown
eyes. *I don't want to know. There's nothing I can do,
nothing I can do about any of it.*

"My wife was eight months pregnant when she was
killed in an auto accident," Michael said, his gaze never
leaving her face.

She closed her eyes. *Fix that, Tess.*

"I'm so sorry," she said. Then she looked at him and
hoped he could see her compassion because she didn't
know how to express it. She'd never been that good
with words.

"It's been a while," he said. She nodded. Yeah, as if
he didn't know the exact amount of time elapsed. "But
when something like that takes me by surprise, it seems
new again. I still never expect it when it happens."

"I'm so sorry," she said again, putting her hand on

his. She didn't know what else to do. But she noticed that he withdrew his hand as discreetly as he could without appearing to reject her comfort. Which was fine because there was nothing she could do about any of it. "It never turns out the way you planned, does it?"

"No," he said. "It never does." He hesitated and said, "Look, Theresa. I really like you. Uh. As a friend. I just—I don't date anymore."

Tess blushed clear to her toes. Had she been that obvious? Of course she had. And the man was still grieving for his lost wife and child. Hadn't Greta warned her? Hadn't Greta said he required handling? Greta hadn't shared the details because it wasn't her place to do so, but Tess could have listened to the warning.

So how should she respond to such a polite brush-off? Clearing her throat, she said, "I appreciate your explaining." Ugh. How awkward. Then, because he was obviously uncomfortable—not to mention how great she felt—she changed the subject. "I finished the cushion. It's in the truck. Here's the invoice."

He took the invoice, set it on the desk, gave it a distracted glance.

"If Jimmy's around, I'll get him to help me carry the cushion in."

Michael nodded without looking at her.

She made her escape.

Tess unlocked the rear doors to the truck and climbed inside. *Just drop the cushion off and go away,* she told herself. She couldn't give Michael his future back. Tears stung at her eyes and she dashed them away. She *liked* Michael. She thought he liked her. She was attracted to him. If he let himself, he might be attracted to her. Why couldn't it be that simple?

Jimmy shuffled his feet impatiently and she dragged her attention back to the task at hand, handing the cushion down, then climbing out of the truck and helping him carry it across the parking lot.

"Don't drop it!" she screeched as he reached behind him to open the rear door to the building. He gave her a look over his shoulder.

"In my line of work," he informed her, "I have actually been known to carry things without dropping them. Many things. In many situations. It's sort of a requirement."

He got the door open, shoved his foot in between it and the frame to keep it propped open, then stuck his hip out to keep the door from closing. Tess watched his contortions with amusement but didn't dare say anything. Then he had the doorstop down and they were able to bring the cushion through. They carried it over to the unfinished settee and plopped it down. Tess worried it into position, then stood looking down at it with a perplexed expression on her face.

"Tell me it looks good," she said to Jimmy.

Jimmy rolled his eyes.

"Jimmy, do you have a girlfriend?"

"Of course."

"Then you understand that women occasionally need reassurance."

"It's beautiful, Tess."

"Why, thank you, Jimmy."

He rolled his eyes again and left her. A moment later she heard the saw start up. She shouted "Thank you!" at Jimmy, who ignored her, then knocked on the door of the office and said briefly to Michael, "All yours."

"Okay."

"Let me know if you want any changes."

Michael glanced up from the computer. "Will do. Thanks."

A pause. "Or you could look at it now to make sure it's okay." That way she wouldn't be summoned here again to fix something he noticed was wrong with it. She would never have to come back here again. Nothing wrong with wanting to avoid intense humiliation. See Tess flee.

"I'm sure it's fine," Michael said.

"Would you just come look at it? I haven't worked for you before, I don't know what you're expecting and I—" *I never want to come back here.* She swallowed the words in the interest of maintaining at least a somewhat professional relationship.

"You're not going to leave until I look, right?"

"Exactly."

He didn't argue further, which she appreciated, just pushed his chair back and followed her out of the office. They walked in silence over to the settee. He looked down at the cushion. "Just as I suspected," he said. "It's fine."

"Thank you," Tess said.

"You want your check now?"

"Sure, if you're feeling that efficient."

"Of course."

Maybe he never wanted her to come back either. At least he was making an effort to act like his normal self. So long as she didn't look into his sad eyes, she was fine. But when she looked into his sad eyes, she wanted to touch his face and smooth some of the pain away, and when had that ever worked? When had she ever fixed anything?

Next stop, serial killers on death row, she reminded herself. She was almost out the door and she never had to come back. That would be best, all things considered. She wanted to cringe, his words echoing in her mind. *I really like you—as a friend.*

"Thanks for the coffee," he said, heading back into the office. "It was really good. I'll have to start indulging in mocha instead of regular." He pulled a checkbook from the desk drawer and scribbled out a check.

"It's my favorite," she said.

He handed her the check. "Tess, I was thinking. Would Belinda like the ark? She seemed very taken with it when she was here. It's a shame for it to just sit in that cabinet if there's a child who'd like to play with it."

"Oh, Michael," she said, swinging around to face him. She couldn't just keep going out the doors after that. She sighed. Well, let it be on his shoulders. It wasn't going to be her fault, whatever happened next. She was trying to get out of there, away from him, before they had to have another conversation about how much he liked her as a friend.

She took a deep breath and said, "Belinda would love it. I could tell she adored playing with it. But are you sure you don't want to keep it for . . . for yourself?" she finished lamely. She winced inwardly. It was a good thing she could draw because she was useless with words.

"I'm sure," Michael said, and he did seem sure. "I should have given it to someone a long time ago."

"She'll love it, Michael. Thank you."

He nodded, his face expressionless, though she knew it couldn't have been easy for him to make the offer. *Discipline,* she thought, and her heart went out to him. If she could just do something . . . "If you want to bring a box and some packing material, you can take it home next time you're here," he said.

Next time I'm here, she thought, a little stunned. *And I almost made it out that door. I was this close.*

"Sounds like a plan," she said.

Maybe she could forget the offer. Then she wouldn't have to go back. But if she "forgot" the offer . . . wouldn't that feel like a stingingly personal rejection to Michael? He'd made the toy for his child, for heaven's sake. It wasn't some piece of plastic he'd picked up on sale at Toys "R" Us for a coworker.

This is always how I get sucked in, Tess reminded herself. She always put herself in the other guys' shoes and asked herself, Tess, how would you feel? And the next thing she knew, she was trying to fix things. She was trying to solve problems that couldn't be solved. Rescuing strays who bit and men who strayed. Proposing to serial killers on death row. No, wait, she hadn't done that. Yet.

She sighed, picking up one of her colored pencils and doodling on the sketchpad that lay open in her lap. No wonder Greta had kept her safely away from Michael all this time. And if Greta hadn't been hurting from the knee surgery and not thinking clearly from the pain medicine, she would never have sent Tess over there, not for any reason.

I have a choice, she told herself. She always had a choice. She was not a victim of her personality. She looked down at the doodles. Hearts. Multitudes of sappy, sentimental hearts. Good heavens. Why not just write *Michael + Tess 4ever*?

"Tess?" Greta said. "What do you think?"

"I think I'm in trouble," Tess said.

"What now?" Greta looked up from her laptop and fixed Tess with a piercing gaze.

Tess glanced at Greta, then shook her head to clear it. She tore the page out of her sketchbook and crumpled it up. "Sorry. I was thinking about something else. What were you saying?"

Greta gave her a dubious look and said, "I was asking

what you thought about shoji screens for the Hendersons' great room. They have all that enormous, unstructured space and it literally echoes when you're in there. We could use screens to define seating groups, game areas, that kind of thing. Remember what we did for the Jungs?"

"The Hendersons have three little kids, don't they? Rice paper shoji screens wouldn't last a minute."

"True." Greta drew her brows together, perplexed, staring hard at the laptop as if it might inspire her.

"I like the sliding screens idea, though," Tess said. "They could close them to create more intimate space and open them for big parties. They entertain a lot, don't they? That's the reason they wanted all the space in the first place. You just can't use rice paper shoji screens, that's all."

"What if we have Michael make some really sturdy sliding screens with fabric panels between the laths?" Greta was thinking aloud. She said the magical name that gave her Tess' complete attention.

I wasn't this ridiculous in high school, Tess thought, remembering those strong, competent hands and how someone was going to have to discuss the project specs with him. And it absolutely wasn't going to be her. *I really like you. As a friend.* How humiliating. She did *not* want to be humiliated again.

"We could make them look like shoji screens," Greta said. "With all those gorgeous black lacquer frames but some pretty, lightweight Asian motif fabric instead of paper."

"That sounds beautiful," Tess said, trying to focus on Greta's problem instead of her own. "But the only type of Asian motif fabric our suppliers carry is that heavy brocade with the woven designs. Couldn't you use a plain cotton?"

"No," Greta said decisively. "Rice paper has body and texture and imperfections that create a kind of design. Besides, thinking about it, I don't want acres of plain fabric in that room. Too bland and boring. You can find something that will work."

"I can?" Tess asked, raising a brow.

"Sure. Find a new supplier."

"Coming up, boss."

"Now, for the flooring . . ."

Chapter Five

"Theresa?"

Tess immediately recognized the husky warm voice on the other end of the line. Plus, Michael was the only one who ever called her that. "Greta's right here," she said, hoping to hand him off before she started fantasizing about him. Again. The man was dangerous to her mental health even when she wasn't in the same room with him.

"Wait—I want to talk to you."

Her heart thudded. *Stop that,* she told herself sternly. *Remember how he wants to be friends?* "What's up?" she asked with a breezy lightheartedness she did not feel.

"I was wondering if you and your daughter would be home tonight?"

"We'll be here at Greta's," Tess said. "We've been having dinner with her since she got out of the hospital, though I think by this weekend she'll prefer being on her own again." She realized she was babbling, which she did when she was nervous, and stopped abruptly.

"I thought maybe it would be a good idea for me to bring the ark to Belinda myself," he said, oblivious to her babbling as well as her nerves. "Then I could tell her about it and she would see I wasn't mad. She might enjoy it more if she knew I really wanted her to have it."

"Sounds fine," Tess said cautiously.

"Would Greta mind if I came over after I'm done here?"

Tess wondered if a bald-faced lie would be discovered. *No, we're repainting the house. I'm afraid not, we all have to wash our hair.* With a sigh, she turned to Greta, who was pretending not to eavesdrop, and said, "Michael would like to stop over after work tonight to give something to Belinda. Okay with you?"

"Of course," Greta said, not looking up from the proposal folder she was putting together. Her lack of interest was deeply suspicious to Tess. What was she up to? The Greta Tess knew and loved would have peppered her with half a dozen questions. Maybe she'd taken a vow of noninterference, like Tess' vow to stop taking in strays.

"That'd be fine, Michael," Tess said to him and hung up before he could do any more damage to her pulse. She could be out of the house when he came over. Let

Greta and Belinda deal with him. They wouldn't mind being friends. Suppose he got finished at 5 P.M. A few minutes to clean himself up, a few minutes to pack the toy, fifteen minutes to get to Greta's house. If she could invent an errand that required her to leave at 5:30 P.M., then she wouldn't have to be in the same room with him.

She took a deep breath and scolded herself. She wasn't in high school anymore. She could manage to be in the same room with a man she had a crush on and not actually fall to pieces. She was a grown-up.

"I'm going to head home," Tess said. "I've got a few things I want to do before I pick up Belinda from school. I was thinking I'd make something simple for dinner, like pasta."

"With that great red sauce you make? Peppers and chorizo sausage?" Greta asked, giving Tess her full attention now.

"You're starting to sound like Belinda," Tess said with a smile. "That's one of her favorites."

"Garlic bread with pesto and a spinach salad with raspberry vinaigrette? Sounds divine."

Well, it had been going to be simple. Boil water, open a jar of spaghetti sauce. But at least preparing Greta's menu would give Tess something to do instead of thinking about Michael and that slow smile and those sad eyes and nothing she could do about any of it.

When she got home, she spent a restless half hour trying to focus on sewing but only managed to mismatch a seam and had to pull it out again. *Concentrate,* she told herself, but then she got up from the machine and shut the door to the sewing closet.

She made herself a cup of tea and treated herself to a piece of the good chocolate she kept on the top shelf, so good she didn't even share it with Belinda. Or Greta.

That made her feel better momentarily. Then she thought of Michael and how that smile was enough to make her give up chocolate and how unlikely it was that he would indulge in eating chocolates when he was feeling at loose ends. He probably did something productive and efficient. The restlessness took hold again. She could teach him how to eat chocolate. She was even willing to share the top-shelf chocolate with him. He'd probably never realize the enormity of such a sacrifice. Jumping to her feet, she paced the tiny living room for a while until it was finally time to pick up Belinda from school and head back to Greta's house.

They stopped by the grocery store to pick up a few of the essentials Greta had requested, Tess declining Belinda's efforts to add everything from pistachios to pastries to the cart. "We have a list, Belinda. We're getting only the things on the list."

"M&Ms on the list?" Belinda said.

Tess showed her the list. "Nope," she said. "Fresh spinach, basil, French bread, green peppers . . . no M&Ms."

"Want M&Ms," Belinda said.

"We'll have dessert at Greta's house," Tess said. "You don't need M&Ms."

"What's for dessert?"

"Ice cream," Tess said, hoping the gallon was still in Greta's freezer.

"M&M ice cream?" Belinda asked hopefully.

"Vanilla," Tess said. "But I'm pretty sure Greta has chocolate sauce."

Belinda tilted her head and studied Tess for a moment. Then she nodded with an air of gravity as if she had reached a decision that ice cream would be an acceptable replacement for M&Ms. Tess felt as if she'd just brokered a weighty deal with a difficult client.

"Watch *Finding Nemo*?"

Give me strength, Tess thought. "Let's not worry about that right now," she said.

"Like *Finding Nemo*."

"I know you do, sweetie. I know you do."

They finally escaped the grocery store—*escaping again,* Tess thought. *What's with me these days?*—and found themselves at Greta's house in no time at all. "Help me with the groceries, please," she said to Belinda as she unbuckled her seat belt and climbed out of the car.

"Why?"

"Say, 'Yes, Mom,' " Tess said.

"Yes, Mom," Belinda said obediently. "Why?"

"Because I need help. Because I asked you to. Because helping other people is polite."

"Oh, okay," Belinda said, climbing out of the car and holding her arms out. Tess deposited a grocery sack in her arms, grabbed the other one herself, and climbed the steps to Greta's front door. Belinda trailed after her, stopping every few feet to examine a bug or remark on a car driving past. Tess had long since learned to tune such things out but she enjoyed talking with Belinda about them—at least when they weren't running late. Which, given Belinda's penchant for stopping to examine bugs or other interesting artifacts of nature every few feet, was pretty often.

"We're here!" Tess called up the stairs to Greta after unlocking the front door and coming into the hallway with Belinda. "We'll be in the kitchen. Yell if you want help."

"Be down in a minute," Greta said.

Tess and Belinda unloaded the sacks on the kitchen counter nearest the sink. Then Belinda—her tongue sticking a tiny bit out of the corner of her mouth as she worked, making Tess want to hug her—folded them and stored them in the recycling bin that Greta kept at the far end of the kitchen.

"Help?" Belinda asked once she'd finished the task.

"Of course you may," Tess said. "Aprons!"

Belinda was already making for the drawer where Greta kept the aprons. She dug one out for each of them. "Belinda is red, Mama is blue," she said, handing Tess the blue apron and pulling the red one over her head, then turning so Tess could tie the bow in back. Tess took the opportunity to give her daughter the hug she'd denied herself earlier.

Then Belinda was washing her hands and demanding that Tess do the same. As Tess dried her hands on the dish cloth, she heard the steady thump of a crutch against the floor, a sound that meant Greta was joining them.

Tess turned expectantly toward the doorway. Greta had one crutch under her arm and was making her way quite competently to the table, where she sat, her injured leg stretched out in front of her. Belinda ran across the floor and threw herself into Greta's arms, remembering at the last moment not to bump into her bad leg.

"Oof," Greta said. "It's good to see you too."

"Did a great job at school," Belinda boasted. "Did good listening."

"Excellent," Greta said. "You know, there are grown-ups who don't do a very good job of listening." Why did Tess get the feeling that comment was directed at her? She threw a glance at Greta, who studiously ignored her.

"Who did you listen to?" Greta asked.

"Played with Elizabeth," Belinda said, ignoring the question. "Peanut butter sandwich for lunch."

"I thought I put ham and cheese in your lunch box," Tess said, getting out the cutting board to chop onions and peppers. The mysteries of the school lunch room.

"What was your lunch?" Belinda asked Greta.

"Your mother wasn't here to fix my lunch," Greta said. "All I had the energy to make was a cup of tea."

"You don't do pathetic very well," Tess said unsympathetically. She rooted through the cabinets until she found the heavy skillet she was searching for. "I noticed you had the energy to be on the phone all day. You could have called if you needed something. Besides, I was here half the morning. Why am I defending myself? And why are your pots and pans never in the same place twice?" she asked.

"Because you always put them away wrong," Greta said. "Then I put them away correctly but you persist in believing they should be where you placed them last."

"I'm the only one who cooks in your kitchen. Why don't you let me put them where I want them?" Tess drizzled a little olive oil into the pan and sautéed the vegetables, then opened a can of tomato paste and mixed everything together.

"Want to do that," Belinda reminded her, so Tess let her add the oregano and minced garlic and other spices.

"We'll let that simmer for a while. Now we can get the bread ready for the oven." Tess warmed a stick of butter between her hands, then started slicing the loaf. "Belinda, why don't you get the spinach out of the refrigerator and wash it."

Not hearing a response, Tess looked up from buttering the bread. Belinda was a few feet from the stove, staring at the skillet. The sauce was bubbling away and she watched the bubbles break.

"Belinda," Tess said gently, setting down the knife. Belinda jerked her head up and looked at her mother. "Can you get the spinach out of the refrigerator? Let's wash it."

"Do it together," Belinda said happily, going to the refrigerator.

Then the spinach was spun dry and ready to be dressed, and the bread was ready to pop in the oven and the water for the pasta was in the saucepan, heating.

"Let's sit here tonight," Greta said, indicating the kitchen table. "I'm tired of spending my life in the bedroom." Tess had thought it impossible for Greta to grow tired of being in the command center but of course she didn't object.

"Sounds good," she said. "Let's set the table, Belinda."

Belinda went to the china cabinet and opened the glass doors as she had done many times before. "How many?" she asked, touching the stack of plates.

"How many people are eating supper?" Tess asked.

"Me and Mama and Aunt Greta."

"How many is that?"

Belinda pointed and counted. "One, two, three."

"That's right. So how many plates do we need?"

"Three plates."

"There you go," Tess said as Belinda lifted three plates from the shelf and brought them over to the table.

When Tess heard the doorbell ring, her belly clenched. She knew who it was. She also knew why he was there—and it wasn't to see her—but that knowledge didn't stop her heart from thudding a little faster. She rinsed her hands quickly, then dried them off and hurried to answer the door. *Slow down,* she chastised herself when she realized she still had the dish towel in her hand. She shouldn't be so quick to meet her doom.

She pulled open the door and Michael smiled at her from the doorstep, carrying a big carton that he handled easily. "Hi, there," he said, and Tess couldn't think how to answer. She just stood looking at him for a while. Then she came to her senses and said, "Oh, I forgot to tell Belinda you were coming. Come in, please."

She showed him into the living room. "Set that down anywhere," she said. He nodded and put the box on the floor near the sofa. "Belinda's in the kitchen." She motioned for him to follow her.

"Belinda," she said as they entered the room. Belinda looked up from placing silverware on the table. "Do you remember Mr. Manning?" Belinda nodded, her eyes wide. She remembered everyone, of course, but what she thought was often something Tess couldn't figure out.

"Hi, Belle," Michael said. The fact the he used her nickname brought a smile to her lips.

"Good," she said.

"So am I," he answered. He glanced at the table and the food bubbling on the stove and said, "Sorry. Didn't realize I was interrupting dinner."

"We haven't started yet," Greta said. "How's it going, Mike?"

"Fine," he said. "How's the knee?"

"I'm surviving," Greta said.

"I'm sure Theresa is taking good care of you," Michael said.

Greta threw up her hands. "I can't get any sympathy around here."

"Do you want to stay for dinner? It's pasta so it's easy to throw on a little more," Tess said, carefully keeping her voice neutral so he wouldn't feel compelled to remind her that they were just friends.

"If you're sure you don't mind," Michael said easily. "All I've got waiting at home is a stale sandwich."

"That's pathetic," Greta said, carelessly disregarding the fact that she never cooked for herself either. "You're a grown man. Surely you've learned how to cook."

"Just because I know how doesn't mean I want to," Michael said, drifting over to the stove where the sauce bubbled merrily and propping a lean hip against the counter. He sniffed the air appreciatively. "Smells good."

"Belinda, grab another plate out of the cabinet," Tess said.

"Why?" Belinda asked.

"Because Mr. Manning is going to stay for supper."

"She can call me Michael."

"Michael is going to stay for supper."

Belinda carefully extracted another plate from the cabinet and bore it ceremoniously to the table. "Sit next to Mama or Aunt Greta or Belle?" she asked.

"Why, I don't know," Michael said. "What do you think?"

"Sit by Aunt Greta," Belinda decided. "On her good side." She put the plate next to Greta's place setting.

"Excellent choice," Michael agreed. "It's wise to stay on Greta's good side."

Tess gave a snort of laughter at his joke, which was the one she'd been making all week and which Greta failed to appreciate. Greta shot her a disapproving look.

"Belinda, I want give you something," Michael said, coming over to the table to talk to her.

"A present?" Belinda asked, eyes shining, abandoning the table setting.

"It's in here," Michael said, gesturing toward the living room, and Tess, seeing Belinda's uncertainty, took her hand. They walked into the room with him. She heard Greta push away from the table to follow them— as usual, her curiosity got the better of her.

Michael knelt on the floor and opened the flaps on the carton. "You remember how you saw the ark at my shop the other day?" he asked Belinda, who drifted over to stand next to him, looking down at the box.

Belinda gave him a puzzled look, then transferred the look to Tess, silently asking for guidance.

"The animals," Tess said.

Belinda's face lit up and she clapped her hands. "The me-mals!" she exclaimed, using the word she hadn't used since she was four or five.

"Right," Michael said. He pulled out a piece of newspaper and unwrapped a wooden figure. "I thought since you liked it so much you should have it."

Belinda reached for the animal he offered, then shot

Tess a glance. "It's okay," Tess assured her, and then the little girl's fingers closed on the animal.

"Ephelant," she said solemnly, turning it over in her hands. "Green and white ephelant."

"It's a beautiful ephelant," Tess said, her heart catching.

"More?" Belinda asked Michael hopefully.

Michael nodded and reached for another handful of newspaper. "I made this ark and these animals for my son a long time ago," he said.

"Who is your son?" Belinda asked, accepting the mate to the first elephant and examining it closely.

"He died," Michael said, pulling another animal from the carton. Tess watched his face but despite the shadows in his eyes, he seemed composed and content to be here, doing this. She let out a little sigh of relief. She hoped Belinda's questions wouldn't prove too painful to him.

"Like Grandpa Nate," Belinda said. "Grandpa Nate died."

"Yes, like Grandpa Nate," Tess said.

"I could have them?" Belinda asked. "The me-mals?"

"Yes."

"He said so?"

Michael tossed Tess a look.

"Your son," Tess said gently. "She doesn't really understand death. I've tried to explain but . . . it doesn't mean a lot to her."

Michael nodded. "My son doesn't mind," he said to Belinda. "I know he'd like you to have them."

"He's sharing," Belinda said to Tess.

Tess glanced at Michael, who had the start of a smile on his face.

"That's right, Belle," he said. "He's sharing."

"That's polite," Belinda said.

Tess opened her mouth to respond but then she heard Michael laugh. She could see the tears in his eyes but he was laughing, so that had to be okay.

"Yes, that's polite," Michael said.

"Help?" Belinda asked, squatting on the floor next to him and digging into the carton to unwrap more animals. Soon newspaper was scattered across the floor and Belinda was sprawled on her stomach, marching the brightly painted animals onto the ark.

"Have you ever heard the story of Noah's Ark?" Michael asked.

Belinda was absorbed with matching the animals to their partners but she looked up and shook her head.

"Noah was—this okay, Tess?" he asked suddenly. "I mean, if you practice Buddhism or something, maybe I should shut up?"

"Nah," Greta said from the doorway. "She practices sleeping in on Sundays."

Tess rolled her eyes. "I don't practice anything," she said. "Go ahead. Tell the story."

Michael nodded, turned to Belinda. "So God told Noah—"

"Who is God?" Belinda asked tranquilly.

"This is going to take a while," Greta said.

Chapter Six

"Greta has a brilliant new idea," Theresa said as she walked into his office the next morning.

Michael tried not to stare. She looked as pretty as ever. Last night had been good—friendly and welcoming, almost as if he belonged at the kitchen table, twirling spaghetti around his fork, listening to Greta and Theresa talk about their days, answering Belinda's innumerable questions, telling them a funny story about a client he was working with. Theresa had practically had to pry Belinda away from the ark to join them at the table. At first, a twinge of sadness had touched his heart, seeing Belinda with the toy, Belinda and not his son, but Tess and Greta made everything seem so easy. Pretty soon he was telling them how he'd made the pieces and why he'd chosen to make Noah's Ark. He'd never thought about why before, and when Belinda asked, he told her that he thought the ark represented hope, and she beamed at him. He didn't know if she understood what he meant. He didn't know if he did, either.

Belinda accepted him so readily that he knew she didn't harbor any ill will about their first encounter, which came as a relief to him because he hadn't meant to hurt her feelings. Last night had been a good occasion. But not one he could repeat, he told himself. It might seem simple—and on the surface it was—but underneath, it was a lot more complicated. Because Theresa wanted more, and he didn't have more, and it wasn't fair to mislead her. In fact, it would be cruel to pretend otherwise. It would only hurt more later.

Theresa took the guest chair on the opposite side of the desk, then pulled the sketchbook out of her bag and put it on the desk. Michael guessed she was being brisk and businesslike. He smiled. Someone should tell her that her blouse wasn't the least bit conducive to businesslike thoughts. He took the desk chair and turned the sketchbook around to face him. Theresa snatched it back and gave him a glare. Unrepentant, he smiled at her and said, "I was just interested in seeing what you've been up to."

"Yeah." She paged to the back of the book, where she'd done a quick sketch. "This is for a series of screens we want to place in an unstructured living space. They're sliding screens—like shoji screens—that we'll install with runners on the ceiling and the floor for stability. We need them to be very sturdy, so we want to use something other than pine. We'll do the whole black lacquer look. Instead of rice paper, Greta wants a thin Asian motif fabric that won't block the light. No idea where I'm going to find that."

She shrugged, setting that problem aside. The shrug dislodged the blouse, which slid precariously down one shoulder. He knew "no" was the kindest thing he could say to her, not to mention to himself, but did she have to make it so hard? Staring at her shoulder, he couldn't have summarized what she'd just said to him on a bet.

Concentrate, he told himself. He'd already told her he wasn't interested, and he meant it. It had been his least favorite conversation of the week. But he wasn't ready to try again. He was never going to be. That part of his life, with all its hopes and expectations, that part was closed.

"Later today, I'm going over to the client's house to take some measurements and get a better sense of the space," Theresa said. "When I have the specs, could you work up a price quote?"

"No problem," Michael said, this time paying attention to her words and not her blouse. He dismissed the question of price in favor of the more interesting question of construction. "We can make the frame in two parts and sandwich the fabric in between." He turned to the computer and tapped in notes. "You'll want a hardwood for the frame. I'll check out a few different options. The finish will be no problem—I know where I can find a high-gloss black paint that will look like lacquer but hold up better. Construction will be a little finicky. You mind if I come with you to look at the space?"

"That's fine," Theresa said, though her expression showed she wasn't thrilled with the idea.

"What are you going to do about the fabric?" he asked. Annoyance flashed in her eyes at his question, but he knew she wasn't annoyed at him. Herself? Greta, for assigning her the task?

"No idea," she said. "I can get plenty of high-quality brocades with an Asian look but nothing as lightweight as we need for this project. I'm going to have to track down a new supplier."

Michael opened his mouth to make a suggestion, then thought better of it. *Stay out of it,* he told himself. He wrestled with some papers on his desk, fiddled with the computer, and then before he could stop himself, he burst out with, "Why don't you design the fabric for the screens? You've got that great dragon sketch that would be perfect for this project." He stopped suddenly, waiting for her reaction before continuing. *Why am I doing this?*

She just stared at him, open-mouthed, the annoyance fading from her face. Then she asked, "How would I get it produced? A minuscule run like that?"

At least she hadn't told him it wasn't any of his business. "You want something really lightweight, right? Why not have the design silk screened onto some unfinished cotton? Or a natural muslin? Something like that. If silkscreening won't work, you could do a hand-blocked print." He didn't know much about fabric design and production but he had handled enough manufacturing difficulties himself to know that there were suppliers who could do almost anything if you broke the problem down right—and had the money to pay for it.

"Huh," Theresa said, looking intrigued. "I never thought beyond becoming a designer. It never occurred to me to go into the production end myself. I suppose I thought it would take tens of thousands of dollars to get started. I never thought about doing specialty short-run work for clients." She thought about it for a moment. "If we did it right, we could offer exclusive or custom designs—at a premium." The glow in her eyes made her even prettier than usual. He found himself leaning forward, leaning into her.

Stop that.

Then she shook her head. "What would I tell Greta? She'd probably go along with it but only because I'd be involved. Not because she thinks it's a great idea."

Michael sensed her discomfort. She'd talked about not wanting to bother Greta before. He didn't think Greta would be bothered, but it wasn't his place to argue. He dropped the subject. If she wasn't interested, she wasn't interested. "So who's the client, where's the house, and when are we meeting over there?"

"This place is huge." Tess and Michael stood in the center of the Hendersons' great room, staring up at the ceiling that arched high above their heads.

"You could rollerblade in here," she agreed.

"I'm not sure I can add runners to the ceiling. Do we really need the screens that tall? I think we should drop them down, maybe to eight feet. Let me see Greta's configuration."

Tess turned to the appropriate place in her sketchbook. She oriented the page to the room and handed it over to him. When he took it from her, she forced herself not to jump back from the electric warmth of his fingers on her hand. He stood close—too close—and the clean, masculine scent of him made her dizzy. *Hello, he wants to be friends,* Tess reminded herself, squirming at the memory of his polite rejection.

"Did you bring your tape measure?" he asked, apparently oblivious to the way he made her breath come unevenly.

"I'm a seamstress," Tess said, digging into her bag and handing it over.

"The implication being that a carpenter ought to have a tape measure too?" Michael grinned. "You are not a subtle woman. Grab that end." He paced off the dimensions of the configurations Greta had planned. Tess noted the actual measurements down in the book.

"What's Greta planning for the flooring?" he asked. "I'll have to install tracks and we'll want to coordinate our efforts."

"She was thinking wood laminate—they've got kids—with a scattering of those thin bamboo area rugs," Tess said. "Keeps the Asian feel going."

"Pergo and black lacquer shoji screens?" Michael asked.

"We do the best we can within the constraints of budget and reality," Tess reminded him. "Hardwood floors and tatami mats would last twelve seconds with this family."

"True. Does Greta have a furniture source? I don't have many Asian furniture designs in my portfolio."

"She's got a line on an East Asian importer," Tess said. "And she'll sneak a few Pier 1 pieces in for budgetary reasons. It'll be fine."

"If anyone can pull it off, Greta can," Michael agreed as he stared up at the ceiling with a frown. Tess glanced over at him. The sound of admiration in his voice stirred a little beast of jealousy in her chest. Why did men always have to admire Greta? Sure, she had a lot going for her, but Tess wasn't exactly without her own charms. If Michael spoke about Tess in that tone of voice, it would make her feel . . . warm. Appreciated. A little of that appreciation and he could do whatever he wanted with her.

You'd let him do whatever he wanted even if he never used that admiring tone about you, Tess scoffed at herself. All he would ever have to do was smile.

"What would you do if you had this space?" she asked, spinning slowly around the echoing space like Belinda might do, curious what his personal taste might be. She'd install skylights and hang weavings, throw fat cushions on the floor and have as much room to spread out and create and live as she and Belinda and the various livestock who lived with them wanted.

"I'd set up hockey nets at either end," Michael said. She stopped and shot him a surprised look. He grinned and added, "I went to college on a hockey scholarship."

"Must have been up north. Not much hockey gets played down here." She eyed him consideringly. His lean, muscular strength appealed to her but she'd assumed it had come from wrestling furniture around. She hadn't figured him for an athlete. He didn't seem—what? Competitive enough?

"I went to the University of North Dakota," he said.

"Cold," she said with a shiver.

"I always managed to find ways to stay warm," he said. Now he had a wicked gleam in his eye that startled and intrigued her. *Much* better, she thought.

"What did you study?" She wanted to keep the sadness out of his eyes for a little while longer.

"Engineering," he replied, another answer that surprised her. "My father was with the Army Corps of Engineers—that's how we ended up in North Dakota when I was in high school—and he liked the work."

"And you became a carpenter because?"

"Because I didn't enjoy engineering as much as my old man did."

"So you're happy being a carpenter? You don't want more than that?" She remembered her ex-husband, always restless, always wanting more, never satisfied, sure she and Belinda were holding him back.

He narrowed his eyes at her and said, "I like my work."

From his expression, Tess realized that she must have offended him, though she wasn't sure how. Changing the subject, she asked, "So what brought you here?"

"My wife," he said briefly, looking away from her. Well, there was never an uncomfortable social situation she couldn't make worse just by trying to make it better.

Don't ask, Tess told herself, looking into his brown eyes. The wicked gleam was gone and that was her fault. *Let it go. Go home and sew something.*

"Did she have family here?" she asked, wishing she hadn't said anything even as she was saying the words. No wonder Belinda asked so many painful questions. She'd learned from her mother. Why was she torturing herself—and probably him—asking questions about his late wife? It was obviously hard for him to talk about her.

"No," Michael said, even more briefly than before, if that were possible. Then he seemed to relent: "She wanted to attend graduate school here."

I wonder how long it's been, she thought. *It still seems incredibly painful to him. She must have been someone amazing.*

"What was she like?" Tess asked. Why not stick a fork in her eye and be done with it?

At first she thought Michael wasn't going to answer.

She waited, tense, for his reaction, but his face was calm and expressionless, so at least he wasn't going to lose his temper. Her ex-husband would have yelled at her for asking too many questions, pushing too hard. When would she ever learn?

Then Michael sighed and said, "Greta reminds me of my wife. She was a beautiful, elegant woman. Interested in art and music. A patron of the Lied Center," he said, referring the city's performing arts center. "She served on all sorts of charitable and volunteer boards. She had a gift for administration and she could make anything run smoothly. She was generous with her time and money."

Tess nodded, staring at him. Something about his words struck her as odd. It wasn't as if he was describing a wife but instead a colleague, someone he knew only on a basic superficial level. Like he was introducing a keynote speaker at a conference. Or reading an obituary.

She shook herself. Of course that's what he sounded like. He wasn't going to share all the warm and intimate details of their life together with her. He obviously admired and respected his wife and missed her with a longing that didn't abate with time. What did Tess hope to accomplish with this conversation?

"She sounds like an amazing person," Tess said, unable to stop herself from getting as many details as possible so she could torture herself with them later. She'd never be the kind of person who served on charitable boards and made anything run smoothly. "What was her name?"

"Vanessa."

Of course. A beautiful name for a beautiful lady. *Am I done asking painful questions?* she asked herself.

"Was it—how long ago did it happen?"

Apparently not.

Another pause and she thought he might ignore the question and she wouldn't have blamed him one bit. Then he said, "Seven years."

Seven years? She sucked a startled breath in. She knew people handled grief differently, but from the way he acted from his refusal to date—not just her but anyone—she would have sworn it had happened only a year or two ago. Vanessa must have been quite a woman. They must have been very much in love for him to be grieving this much, so many years later. What kind of love, when lost, would turn Michael into the kind of man who would never pursue another relationship, never fall in love again, never take another shot at marriage? Hopelessly devoted to a dead woman's memory?

Remember this, Tess told herself sternly. To him, it was yesterday that his wife died. Tess didn't stand a chance of getting his attention now.

Michael couldn't get out of the Hendersons' house soon enough. It wasn't that Theresa had to ask all those wrenching questions about his wife and he had to answer calmly, so she wouldn't know the truth. That inquisition hadn't bothered him half as much as her infuriating off-hand comment about his being a carpenter.

He should have known, he thought as he shoved the truck into gear. He didn't even glance back to see Theresa standing by her car door, staring after him with a pain-filled expression in her eyes. He didn't care if she felt bad. She should. He'd believed that she might be different, but she wasn't. *Don't you want more?* How often had he heard that in his life? As if what he was doing was secondhand, second-class. Not enough. He owned his own business. He enjoyed his work. He had more orders than he could reasonably handle and he'd have to hire another assistant soon. But none of that mattered. Because he didn't wear a suit and tie to work, what he did was dismissed. Who he was didn't matter.

His carpentry work was admired, he made a good living, he was in charge of how and when and for whom. Yet he was supposed to want "more"? Like what? An impressive title, a biweekly paycheck, a tedious commute, a bullying boss, a rigid nine-to-five schedule, work he despised? Would that be "more"?

His tires kicked up gravel as he roared into the parking lot of his shop. He was disappointed. No, he admitted, he was angry. Angry in a way that he hadn't been in a long time. Not since . . . *betrayed,* that was how he felt. He'd really thought Tess was different. He'd thought she had an imagination, that she wouldn't be like other women who thought lawyers and doctors and engineers were "better" than carpenters. He'd thought more of her than that. Even as the anger sparked through his veins, he wondered why he cared. Theresa wasn't anything to him. A business colleague, that was all. Who cared what she thought?

Apparently he did, and that made him even angrier.

"What's got your goat?" Jimmy demanded when Michael slammed shut the door to the workshop. He abandoned the lunch he was eating at one of the workstations to stare at Michael.

"You ever want more?" Michael asked, his tone savage.

"You offering a raise, man?" Jimmy responded equably.

"No, I'm just asking if you're satisfied being a carpenter."

"I like it." Jimmy took a long swallow of Coke, wiped his mouth with the back of his hand and shrugged.

"And Tiffany? What does Tiffany think?" Michael ran agitated fingers through his hair.

"Tiffany thinks I'm employed, which is a big step up from her last boyfriend. What's biting you, man?"

"I'm through with women," Michael said, quashing the strong desire to throw something. Maybe Jimmy.

"You've been through with women as long as I've known you," Jimmy said. "What happened? Tess hurt your feelings?"

"Shut up," Michael growled, immediately deflated by Jimmy's sarcasm.

"When you're looking for a reason to run the other way, any reason will do," Jimmy remarked, turning his attention back to his ham sandwich.

"Wait a minute," Michael said. "I'm supposed to be the voice of wisdom here."

"Yeah. What does the voice of wisdom always tell me when I give up on Tiffany?"

"I say, 'dump her,' " Michael said disagreeably.

"You do not," Jimmy said, letting out a burp. He smacked his chest with his fist and said, "You always tell me, 'Talk to her, man. Find out what she means.' I seen the way Tess looks at you."

So had Michael. The heat flared in his veins at the thought of it.

"So talk to her, man," Jimmy said. "Find out why she did or said whatever it is that's chafing you."

"You may be right," Michael said, staring at the other man. When had that ever happened before? "You may be right."

For the next day or two, Tess threw herself into finishing up several small jobs for Greta and spending extra time with Belinda. When Michael called about the shoji screens, she handed the phone directly to Greta.

"Michael gave me his quote," Greta said after she hung up the phone. "I just need to know the cost of the fabric so I can get the proposal to the Hendersons. I'd like to get that done this week." An implied criticism in her tone made Tess feel defensive, even though Greta was basically asking the impossible.

"I haven't found a supplier yet," Tess said.

"Could you make it a priority? I want to get this put together. I'm pretty sure the Hendersons will agree to our plans but I don't want them to cool off."

"I'm on it," Tess said before Greta could start in on her other platitudes, such as striking while the iron was hot and how a stitch in time saved nine. Tess didn't even point out that she'd already made it a priority, with nothing to show for the effort. Instead, she went home and made a series of phone calls to silk screen companies. She learned that, just as Michael had suggested, she could readily have her design silk-screened on a small yardage. If she converted the sketch to a design in a graphics program and sent it to the production company, they'd charge a onetime setup fee and then could supply her with small amounts of yardage of the design at any time at a set price per yard. She'd used graphics programs when she was earning her art degree, so that was no problem. But coming up with the money for the setup fee and the initial print run was way beyond her budget even though it wasn't the tens of thousands of dollars she'd originally thought she'd have to invest.

She knew if she asked Greta, she would be supportive, because Greta always was, but not necessarily because she thought it was a good idea. Plus, Greta had enough expenses right now without Tess asking her to scrape together the money for the initial setup fee and print run. Health insurance wouldn't cover all the costs of her knee surgery and rehab, plus there was no paid time off for the self-employed. Being unable to do on-site consultations right now limited the work Greta could bring in and the number of new clients she could take on, and that meant she'd have cash flow difficulties down the road. Tess didn't want to add more financial stress. More important, Tess wanted to do it on her own. Just once, do something right without Greta having to help her or to save her.

She closed the phone book and looked at her jotted notes in the back of her sketchbook. Then she sighed and started calling another ten fabric suppliers to see if she could locate the kind of material Greta wanted.

Tess sat at one of the small marble-topped tables at La Prima Tazza, sipping a mocha and staring out the window. She didn't feel like going to work and talking to Greta, who was going to ask her about finding fabric suppliers. Tess would tell Greta she couldn't find one but that wasn't going to stop Greta, who was going to pester her to the brink of insanity.

As she stared, she spotted the rangy figure striding down the sidewalk. A moment later, Michael pulled open the door to the coffee shop. Their eyes met and Tess felt that familiar sizzle in the pit of her stomach. *This is so unfair,* she thought, fighting down the sizzle.

"Hi, Michael," she said, and her voice sounded breathless even to herself. Michael returned the greeting with the smile she always found herself waiting for.

He got his coffee—a mocha, Tess noted. Not quite sure what that meant, but she told herself it didn't mean *no* had turned into *yes*. Then he was next to her, asking if he could join her at her table. She nodded—*why?*—and scooted over so he could take a chair.

"No sketchbook this morning?" he asked. She raised an eyebrow. He must have seen her in here sometimes, working on her designs. But they hadn't known each other then. Had there really been a time when she hadn't known him? It didn't seem possible.

"Not this morning," Tess said in response to his question. "This morning I'm avoiding Greta."

"Because?"

"Because I can't find a supplier for the fabric she has delusions of using for the Hendersons' screens. I've called at least twenty-five places all over the country, and scoured the Internet for leads. Nada."

Michael took a sip of his coffee. "The solution seems simple," he said. "Why not do it yourself?"

"I looked into it," Tess said, "but I can't afford the setup costs and I don't want to ask Greta for the money. I know she doesn't have it to spend and I don't want her to get into debt because I had an idea." Tess glanced at him. "Actually, it was your idea. But I'm the one who wants to be the designer."

"How much?" Michael asked. His dark gaze penetrated her hastily erected wall of indifference. All of his attention and energy was focused on her. It was flattering but also overwhelming. There was so much of him—breadth and heat and presence. Her awareness of him hummed along her nerves. She desperately tried to keep her mind on the conversation. What had he asked? How much.

"More than I can spend," she said.

"How much?" he repeated patiently.

Tess sighed and told him.

"That sounds reasonable," Michael said. He sat back in his chair, as if some tension had been released.

Her shoulders immediately tightened, as if his released tension had been absorbed by her. "Sure, if you have more than twelve dollars saved," Tess retorted.

"Have you thought about finding someone to invest in your idea? As a business?"

Tess shrugged. He made it sound simple and she knew it was anything but. She tried to marshal her arguments. "Since it would be a part-time business, and not likely to turn much profit, I can't really imagine who'd invest. Not a bank, that's for sure. And even if I could find an organization willing to loan the money, it would take months to write a business plan, find a lender, get the money. I need the fabric now."

"What about a private investor?" he persisted.

Was this how people felt when she asked her annoyingly persistent questions? "My family wouldn't help," she said, knowing where he was headed and not sure how she felt about it. "My friends are all in the same boat I'm in—they don't have any extra funds to invest, even if they did think it was a great idea."

"What about me?" Michael asked. "I'm your friend, right?"

"You're someone I do business with," Tess corrected, then wished she hadn't when she saw the smile leave his face. But he wasn't her friend, not really. He couldn't be, not with the way she felt about him, not with the way he'd made it clear there would never be anything more between them.

"Even better," he said, though he didn't sound like he meant it. "We can do business together."

"I'm not sure that's a good idea," Tess said. In fact, she was sure it was a bad idea.

"Why not? Your designs are excellent. Even I can see that, and I'm not trained in the field. You could start with silk screened and hand blocked pieces, and then when your business started turning a profit, you could look into producing woven and printed designs." His eyes were intense, not sad, and his face animated with interest as he tried to convince her of the benefits of his plan. "You know Greta would love to have access to exclusive and custom designs that no one else in the neighborhood would have."

Why did he have to be so appealing? Why couldn't he be sixty-two, bald, and pot-bellied? She'd be his friend then and it wouldn't bother her to accept an investment from him. But her feelings were too mixed up. She wasn't certain she could make a good judgment about his offer. Of course when had *Tess* and *good judgment* ever gone together in the same sentence anyway?

"Don't you think?" he prompted.

"I suppose," Tess said cautiously. She didn't want to be responsible for putting the sadness back in his eyes by issuing a unilateral *no,* but she'd never imagined starting her own business. On the other hand, Michael owned his own business, and if he was willing to help, maybe it wouldn't be so impossible after all. She eyed him over the coffee cup. The question was, did she want to continue tangling with him? Because if he loaned her money and advised her on the business she was contemplating, then she was going to have to keep seeing him, talking to him, dealing with him. A sensible woman would pass up the opportunity to get her heart stepped on. For example, Greta would never sit here waiting for her heart to break.

"You could start with this project," Michael said. "We know what the initial costs are. Then we add a premium for the design and overhead plus a little profit for both of us. Have you got a pen?"

His enthusiasm, which she'd never quite encountered like this, was contagious. In a daze of conflicting thoughts—she wanted to but she was scared—Tess dug in her bag for the sketchbook and pencils she brought with her everywhere. She handed them over, then scooted around to sit closer to Michael at the table.

"We'll need about fifty yards for the screens," she said. "The basic cotton we can use costs about five dollars a yard wholesale." She sounded perfectly under control and businesslike. Must have come from all those years of watching Greta.

Michael made a note in the sketchbook. "We know the silk-screening charges," he said, writing down the numbers Tess had quoted him earlier. "We need to calculate a fee for your design and build in compensation for project management." He gave her an expectant look.

"I'll have to convert the design to a digital file," she said. "And I may need to buy a program to be compatible with the silkscreen company's computers. Then there are just a few chores: transmitting the file, verifying they received it correctly, getting the sample approved."

Michael nodded and jotted more figures down. His face looked absorbed as he worked, the lines of tension smoothed away.

I am in so much trouble, Tess told herself, turning to stare blindly out the window. There could have been a circus on Massachusetts Street—there often was, of one kind or another—and she wouldn't have noticed it.

"Tess?"

She glanced over at him with a start.

"Look at the numbers," he said. "Can you charge that much per yard? That will repay my initial investment, give us both a little something for our time, and leave you with enough money to fund your next print run." He gave her his slow smile and her heart turned over in her chest. He made it sound so reasonable, so possible.

"That's if the Hendersons like the design," she reminded him. "We'll have to produce a sample before they give final approval. That means we have to pay for everything up front. What if the Hendersons hate it?"

"They won't hate it."

"You don't know that."

He shrugged, unconcerned. "All investments have an element of risk."

"I'm not going to let you lose all your money on this."

"It's not *all* my money," Michael said. "I wouldn't offer if I didn't think it was a good bet."

She believed him. Unlike Greta, he had no underlying motives. He wasn't trying to impress her or win her heart. It was his idea to invest, not hers. She hadn't asked him for any favors.

"We need a written agreement." She bit her lip as she thought about it. "And it will include repayment terms if the initial run doesn't sell."

He studied her for a moment. "A risk-free investment sounds like a good idea to me."

"Don't be patronizing," she said. "It's not risk free. You don't know that I'll repay you even with terms written into the contract." Thinking about it made her stomach hurt. How would she pay him back if she failed? He was offering her a chance to do what she wanted to do, dreamed of doing. How much had she risked—and lost—for other people? Why not take a risk on herself? Just once?

She rubbed her sweating palms against her jeans. She could do it. She wouldn't even think of failing.

"Okay," she said. "Okay."

His only reaction was a brisk nod. "Why don't you give that quote to Greta and then if she gets approval to go ahead with the design, I'll write you a check so you can get started."

"Okay," she said again. Her hands shook with anxiety and excitement. Maybe she really could do this. "I'll let you know what happens. And thanks, Michael."

"No problem," he said. He looked at his empty coffee cup. "I should get to work."

Tess nodded, then put a hand on his arm as he rose to go. At her touch, he stopped abruptly. She pulled her hand away quickly, flustered and embarrassed. Michael didn't say anything, just looked at her. "I wanted to tell you Belinda has really enjoyed the ark," she said in a rush. "I appreciate your letting her have it."

"No problem," Michael said again, which seemed to be his standard response to most things. Then he was slipping out the front door. Watching him go, Tess felt a pang. He looked so alone as he walked down the sidewalk.

That was his choice, she told herself firmly. There was nothing she could do about his problems. And despite the fact that he seemed more involved in her life than he should be, they weren't going anywhere. He'd made that perfectly clear. She wasn't going to get involved. She wasn't going to care. He was still mourning his dead wife and son and she would just get hurt if she thought they could be anything more than two people who did some work together. So why did the day suddenly seem so flat and lifeless without him in it?

Michael climbed into his truck but he didn't start the ignition right away. He sat looking at the coffee shop. Behind that glass door, Theresa was finishing her coffee, maybe drawing a design, thinking about the business she was starting. Soon she'd come out and get into her car and head home, if she had sewing to do, or to Greta's, if they had other work to discuss.

From their conversation, he knew she didn't have much money, so he supposed she and Belinda lived in a small rental property. Even so, he knew Theresa would have fixed it up with paint and fabric and flowers. You wouldn't notice how old the appliances were or that all the furniture came from yard sales.

Vanessa hadn't been like that. The thought of his late wife going to a yard sale brought an unwilling smile to his face. They couldn't be more different. If he'd tried to find the exact opposite of Vanessa, Theresa would be it.

He hadn't been able to have the conversation he'd wanted to have with Theresa, as Jimmy had advised, but he wasn't angry or frustrated now. He didn't know what to think about himself or her. What had possessed him to push her so hard on the design business? What did it matter to him? And to agree to invest in it. Where had that idea come from? Not that he couldn't spare the money, just that he'd certainly had no such intention when saw her sitting at the table and had decided to go inside to get a cup of coffee and talk with her.

Yet something made him insist on giving her the loan. It wasn't because she was such a nice person. It wasn't that he thought of her as a kid sister he was offering a hand to. No. Nothing as simple or as generous as that. He'd done it so that their lives would stay entwined. Because for the first time in years, life outside his workshop had gotten interesting. A smile quirked his lips. Other men would ask for a dinner date. He suggested a business partnership. The smile disappeared as he remembered why he wouldn't ask for a dinner date.

On the heels of that thought came another unwelcome one: how much he'd like to be in the coffee shop with Theresa instead of out here in his truck. He sighed and started the truck. Soon Theresa would come out the door of the coffee shop and he'd feel really idiotic if she caught him staring at her like she was his last hope.

Chapter Seven

Michael switched off the sander and set it down, then picked up a soft cloth to brush the sawdust off the table he was prepping. Sugarland was blasting from the stereo system. He would have preferred something quieter but it was Jimmy's day to pick. Jimmy was hammering a cedar porch swing together. Between the blows, he was talking to Michael. All of which did not lend itself to pointless daydreaming about a dark-haired woman with flashing eyes. But still he managed it.

"And then Tiffany says, 'You never take me anywhere,' and I say, 'I take you to Applebee's all the time,' and she says, 'But we never do anything fun!' And I say, 'We go bowling every Wednesday.'" Jimmy shook his head and pounded another nail into the poor defenseless wood. Michael had tried to explain that if you wanted to be a fine carpenter, you couldn't take your emotions out on the wood, but Jimmy still hadn't learned to leave his frustrations aside. He'd either learn or find another line of business, Michael knew. In the meantime, Michael kept him busy with the rougher work.

"Why didn't you just ask what she wanted?" Michael asked mildly, smoothing a hand over the tabletop. Hadn't they just had this conversation, with Jimmy advising Michael?

"I did!" Jimmy said. "I did it, man. I said, 'So why don't you tell me what you want to do?' and she goes, 'I wanna go dancing, Jimmy.' And I am not a dancer. Is George Strait a dancer? Is Toby Keith a dancer?"

"I'm guessing no?" Michael said. One more coat of varnish and the table would be perfect. Perfect. The client would hand over a fat check, but that wasn't the point. The point was that you could create a thing of beauty. You could step back and see that you'd made art. Even if it was a kitchen table. The beauty, the art, was a reward for staying in control. Disciplined. Efficient. Focused. Could he please remember that the next time he thought of straying from his orderly, productive life?

"I bet they dance the-two step," a lilting voice said from the doorway. Both men turned to stare at the source. *Theresa.* Should have known from the disturbance in the air.

"What?" Jimmy asked. At least one of them was capable of speaking. Michael's own mouth was suddenly dry and he'd run out of things to say. Not that "What?" was particularly erudite.

Michael couldn't help staring. She was wearing a white blouse with colorful flowers embroidered around the scoop neckline. It was falling off one shoulder and she shrugged it back into place with a movement that made him dizzy. He actually started to move forward without conscious thought. He made himself stop. Vanessa would never have worn a shirt like that. She would have looked ridiculous in it.

"Two-step. You know? One-two, quick, one-two, slow," Theresa was saying, setting two cups of coffee down on one of the workstations. "I'm sure George Strait and Toby Keith do the two-step. I've seen Tim McGraw do it," she expanded on her theme. She might as well have been speaking another language for all Michael was comprehending. Unable to trust himself, he stood rooted to the spot, unspeaking.

"Huh," Jimmy said, setting the hammer down and giving her a speculative look. "Is it hard to learn?"

"It's simple," Theresa said. "It takes about ten seconds to learn and then all you have to do is practice a little. It's so romantic to dance the two-step. I'm sure your girlfriend won't mind you stepping on her toes as long as you're on the dance floor with her."

"You don't know my girlfriend," Jimmy warned.

"You got any classic country around here?" she asked, gesturing at the stereo. "Some of that George Strait you were talking about?"

"Sure." Jimmy walked over to the rack by the stereo and pulled out a couple of CDs. As he slotted George Strait into the player, Michael saw the chagrined expression on Tess' face, like she'd just realized it was too late to back out now, regretting that she'd even opened her mouth. Well, Jimmy was dusty, sweating, and shirtless, so maybe that had something to do with her hesitation. Michael bit back the urge to demand that Jimmy put his shirt on before Theresa touched him.

Then George was singing, and she held out her hands to Jimmy.

"This should be interesting," Michael said, setting down the cloth to watch, relieved to find that he was capable of speech after all. When he realized his hands had curled into fists, he shoved them into his pockets.

"Okay. Here's how you hold your partner." She demonstrated.

"Got it," Jimmy said.

"Now, if it's someone you don't know very well, such as myself, you leave some personal space between the two of you." She took a half-step back. "There. Now take one step to the right with your right foot and slide your left foot along after it. Okay. Now another step. See? One, two. Make them quick. Okay, now with your left foot, take a step to your left, sliding your right foot along behind. Then another step. Make them slow."

"Okay," Jimmy said doubtfully, doing as she instructed. He was probably stepping on her toes but Michael's attention wasn't on their feet. It was on the sway of her hips under her skirt.

"Two steps forward, two steps back," she explained. "It's the epitome of all that is country music."

Jimmy grinned. "Gotcha."

"Now, you want to be in time to the music," she said. "Here we go. See how simple that is?"

"That's all I have to do?" Jimmy said. "One-two, one?"

"That's it."

"So when George comes on, I hold out my hand and say, 'Would you like to dance?' and then we just do this?"

"Yep. And even if she doesn't know the two-step, you'll just lead and she'll follow and it will be fine."

"What if they don't play George?"

"They'll play George. If you go to a country night-club, I guarantee they'll play George."

"But if they don't?"

"You can two-step to anything."

"Yeah?"

"Anything. You just have to find the rhythm. It's in every song ever written. Harder to find sometimes than others but it's there. Sometimes it's slower, sometimes it's faster. But two-stepping isn't about the dance or the music anyway."

"It's not?"

"Nope. The two-step is about the person you're dancing with."

"Huh."

"Yep. See, it's the dance you use to get a little closer to someone. You start out here," she indicated their position. "And who knows where you'll end up?"

"Huh," Jimmy said. "Wish I'd known about this a long time ago."

"Let me show you. Start out here with your girlfriend. Then you pull her a little closer."

Jimmy tugged on her waist, her cotton skirt flaring as she moved. Michael watched it and thought, *She's flirting with me and she's not even looking at me. She can flirt with her back turned.* He ran a shaking hand over his face. *I am so not ready for this.*

"Smooth." Theresa laughed at Jimmy's antics. "You can be more subtle than that."

"Let me try again."

"Okay." She took a step back. Then he slid his arm around her waist, guiding her closer, his hand sliding down her back. She smacked his hand away. Good thing or Michael would have done it for her.

How would it feel to hold her close like that? He swallowed hard. He could guess how it would feel. A woman like Greta would keep her distance, enjoying the dance, teasing, never letting him get too close. Theresa . . . Theresa would melt against him, warm and soft. *Nothing wrong with that.*

"There you go," Theresa said to Jimmy. "You're a fast learner."

"I'm getting the hang of it," he said.

"Now hush, here's "Amarillo by Morning." If they play this while you're dancing with her, she won't even complain that you're stepping on her toes. You know what, request it."

"This? I've always hated this one. He's bleating like a lovesick sheep."

"Do not criticize George Strait," she said severely. "Listen. This is such a romantic song."

"Women," Jimmy said. But he slid his hand along her waist and pulled her closer. She closed her eyes, letting the music drift over her as they danced. Then he slid his other hand onto her back and she linked her arms around his neck, resting her cheek on his shoulder.

In that moment, Michael wanted to club Jimmy over the head and take his place. Michael knew exactly what she was doing. Flirting by proxy. *The two-step is about the person you're dancing with,* she'd told Jimmy. But Michael knew perfectly well that this two-step was about the person Theresa *wasn't* dancing with.

"Wow," Jimmy said after a moment.

"You see what I mean?" Theresa said, pulling away from him. "You start over there and who knows where you'll end up."

"Can we get back to work?" Michael snapped, then immediately regretted his betraying tone. What was wrong with him? She was just showing Jimmy how to dance. Someone had once shown Michael how to dance. Why was he getting frustrated and annoyed by it?

Because he wanted to take Theresa into his arms like

that but didn't dare and there was Jimmy getting what Michael wanted and Jimmy wasn't even trying. Jimmy didn't even want it.

"Sure. I'm all through here," Theresa said.

"You came here to show Jimmy how to two-step?" Michael inquired.

"No, but I think it's a good day's work, don't you?" she grinned, pushing her curly dark hair away from her face. It was all he could do not to whimper with longing. If Jimmy hadn't been in the room, Michael knew he would have done something rash.

"Remind me why you're here?" he grated out.

Michael didn't usually look quite so bleak and forbidding. Maybe he had something else on his mind, Tess thought, taking an involuntary step back. "The sample?" she reminded him. "You said you'd write a check."

He seemed to shake himself and when he looked at her again, his expression was calm and friendly.

"You got the go-ahead? Congratulations. Didn't I tell you?" His voice was warm and husky, his words kind and sincere. She must have imagined or misunderstood that other look.

"Thanks," she said. "I wrote up a letter of agreement for you to take a look at."

He nodded. "Let's go into my office."

She grabbed the coffee she'd brought and followed him in. Given her susceptibility, she was grateful for his businesslike approach and hoped he'd dropped the idea of their being friends. She handed him his cup of coffee. Of course, it would probably help if she'd stop doing friendly things. Then he would have no reason to misconstrue their relationship or think he had to set her straight about it. Not that they had a relationship. Whatever the thing was that they had between them. Understanding and longing and loneliness. For all she knew that was already a relationship. Just not the one she wanted.

"Mocha?" he asked, taking the cup. Then he smiled and her heart lurched again.

"Mocha," she confirmed and smiled back at him. Taking a deep breath, she pulled the letter she'd printed out from her bag. "I didn't try to make it sound too legal," she said. "I figured that was likely to backfire on someone who hasn't been to law school. I just wrote down what we talked about last week."

Michael unfolded the sheet of paper she handed him. He squinted at it, then glanced at her and opened his top desk drawer. Producing a pair of reading glasses, he put them on his nose and proceeded to read.

"You're as bad as Greta," Tess said with the amusement of someone still in possession of twenty-twenty vision, then fell quiet as he concentrated on reading the letter. After a few minutes, he opened the top drawer again and folded the glasses away. Then he found a pen in the container on the corner of his desk and signed the letter, handing it back to her. "That's fine," he said. The phone rang and he glanced over at the instrument but didn't answer it.

"Here's a second copy for you," Tess said, pulling another sheet of paper from her bag. Michael took it, glanced at it, and added it to a pile on his desk. He looked at her for a minute, then seemed to shake himself, as if he'd remembered why she was sitting there. He scrabbled in another drawer, came out with a checkbook and wrote out a check. Then he handed it to her. "Knock 'em dead," he said.

"I really appreciate it," she said. That didn't seem like much of an expression of gratitude. She shook herself. Would she worry about expressing gratitude to her banker? Absolutely not. She just needed to think of Michael as her banker. She was here to do a little banking, that was all.

She put the check away in her bag without looking at it. She knew it was for exactly the amount they had agreed on. Wait a minute. Would she think that about her banker? No, she'd check to make sure the loan proceeds were as stated. But the moment had passed and she couldn't very well take the check out of her bag and look at it now. Even when she was trying to simplify, she made things more complicated. "Thanks so much," she said with a sigh.

"No problem," Michael said, just as she'd expected him to.

She sat for a moment but couldn't think of anything else to say. He seemed to be waiting for her lead, sipping his coffee and watching her. Finally, she said, "I'll let you get back to work."

"Yeah, with that Henderson project I'm going to be working twelve-hour days for the next little while." But he made no move to get up and go back to work. So she stood and held out her hand. Banker, she reminded herself. He looked at her hand for a moment, then seemed to realize she expected him to shake it. He did so, giving her a look she couldn't quite interpret. "Let me know how everything goes," he said.

"No problem," she said.

"What is *that*?" Jimmy asked when Michael returned to the workshop to finish sanding the table. "I can smell it from here."

"This? Mocha coffee."

"I'm sorry, I thought you said you were drinking chocolate coffee?" Jimmy said. "What is wrong with you, man?"

"I like it," Michael said mildly.

"You had a call while you were in your, uh, conference," Jimmy said, shaking his head in pity and picking up his eye protection. "Your mother is coming for a visit."

"I'm going to need something stronger than this," Michael said, looking sadly at the cup of coffee.

On Friday, Tess got the phone call from the silk screener saying the sample was ready. It had only taken three days, but even though it wasn't long, she hadn't slept, but tossed and turned, spending hours staring at the ceiling, hoping she hadn't taken Michael's money to finance a disaster, fearing that she had done just that.

She drove into Kansas City, where the silk screen company was located. She picked up the wrapped sample, which she didn't dare look at until she was in the car by herself. Then she carefully peeled back the paper wrapping and squinted, taking it in slowly in case it had turned out terribly wrong.

A dragon's wing . . . a little blurrier than she'd expected, the contrast between the colors not as strong as she'd thought. But since they were going to be using yards and yards of the material, that was probably a good thing. She wanted the design to attract attention, but then fade into the background. She wanted people to catch sight of the design now and then and smile at discovering a new piece of whimsy they hadn't noticed before, but she didn't want the fabric to dominate the space.

She unfurled the piece of fabric and draped it over the steering wheel, picking out the different dragons. Then she held the sample up to the light. The sun glowed through, but the dragons were still faintly visible. Just as she and Greta had discussed.

She stared at the fabric for a little while longer. It was good, she told herself. It really was good. Then she took a deep breath and started back to Lawrence. She had to show it to Michael. He would be as pleased as she was.

"Here it is," Theresa said, barging through the double doors to the workshop. Michael looked up from the chair he was bending over, trying to fit a joint together. Somehow even though he wasn't thinking about her, he was aware when she wasn't there. And then when she was . . . everything seemed better. Even if it had been just fine before. The thought was faintly alarming. When had he ever met a woman who could improve everything?

Despite the air-conditioning system working as hard as it could, the heat in the workshop was overpowering and he'd taken his shirt off while he worked on the chair. He was dripping sweat. This was nothing unusual in his line of business. It was only when Theresa stared at him that he became aware that he was only half-dressed. He couldn't think of anything to say. Apparently neither could she. He hoped that was a good sign, and not evidence that she was overcome with disgust.

After a while, he said, "I'm just joining these two pieces together," which wasn't exactly sparkling repartee but at least he'd managed to squeeze a few words past his throat. Theresa nodded, swallowing hard. A small glow of satisfaction started in his belly. There was nothing so discouraging as being the only one in the room who was finding it hard to speak.

Michael turned his attention back to his work, then clamped a towel in a vise and screwed the vise in place to hold the pieces securely until the glue dried. Then he straightened and came over to her. "What have you got?" he asked, smiling at her. She always made him want to smile.

She took a small step backward as he drew closer. "Sorry," he said. "I've been sweating over this project all morning. I'll try not to drip on you." He could see the pulse hammering in her throat.

"That's not it," she whispered, and despite all his solemn vows to keep this strictly business, his smile widened. She never looked at Jimmy like this and he barely ever wore a shirt. "Never mind," she said firmly, and he knew she'd made a solemn vow too. "Look." She held out a length of fabric.

"My hands are dirty. Set it down over there so I can take a look." He pointed to an unfinished table that was waiting for a coat of stain. She spread the fabric out on it and he came over to see. He was pleased—and relieved, he had to admit—that the sample had turned out so well. He turned to her and said, "It's . . . well, beautiful isn't exactly what you're going for, but it is beautiful. Turned out softer looking than I was expecting, but for those screens, that's what we want."

"That's what I thought," Theresa said. "I think it looks pretty good."

"It's perfect. But you know that."

"Now I just have to show it to Greta and hope she and the Hendersons like it."

"You haven't shown it to Greta yet?" he asked. He was surprised that she'd come here first before she even showed the material to Greta. Surprised and touched.

"You're my partner on this deal," she said lightly. "I wanted you to see it before anyone else did."

"I appreciate that," he said, meeting her gaze, his voice deepening as he looked at her. He could drown in those dark, flashing eyes—

No. No, he couldn't. He yanked hard at his self-control and said, "You should be proud of yourself."

She gave him that flirty smile. Did she know how that smile made him feel? Was that why she did it? "Wish me luck," she said. "I'm off to Greta's house."

"You won't need luck."

"You ever have a girlfriend, man?" Jimmy said from over Michael's shoulder.

Michael glanced up, startled. "Didn't hear you come back from lunch."

"You were busy," Jimmy said, his tone speaking multitudes of comments he didn't have to say to communicate. "Now give the girl some reassurance."

"Shut up," Theresa said, but she was grinning at him.

"Greta's going to love it," Michael said.

"Thanks."

"Hey, that two-step worked, Tess," Jimmy said, punching her on the shoulder. "It was awesome! She loved it.

I did what you said, I requested George Strait, and they played it. And everything went just like you said it would."

"Glad it worked," she said.

Jimmy leaned closer to see what they were inspecting. "That's cool!" he said, his eyes widening. "That's really cool."

Michael saw Theresa's face brighten at Jimmy's comment. First the kid was dancing with her, then he was cheering her up with his enthusiasm. Michael was going to have to fire him, that was clear. Or else learn something from him.

"That sample came, Greta," Tess called out as she let herself in her sister's front door. She reminded herself to act the way she always did, so she went into the kitchen and poured a glass of water—hot out there—and drank it down, no hurry. Then she went to the foot of the stairs and called up, "Do you need anything while I'm down here?"

"Could you make me a cup of tea? That'd be great," Greta said.

Tess tapped her foot with impatience as the water boiled. It was fine to act naturally but she was itching to show the sample to Greta. What would Greta think about the fabric? If she hated it, what would Tess say to Michael? *Banker,* she reminded herself. What would she say to her banker? A banker wouldn't have loaned the money in the first place, so she had no idea. At least she'd promised to pay the money back, though how she'd manage that on top of her other bills, she wasn't sure. She'd find a way. She always did.

Finally the water boiled. She poured the hot water into the mug and dunked a tea bag in it. Then she tucked the wrapped fabric under her arm and brought it and the mug upstairs with her. She put the mug down on the nightstand next to Greta, then tossed the package of fabric on the bed. Casually. She didn't care, right? Made no difference to her.

Greta frowned over something on her laptop. "This business would be more enjoyable if there were actually a profit margin in it," she grumbled, then shook her head and set the laptop aside. "This it?" she asked, pulling the package toward her.

"That's it." Tess' heart hammered in her chest but she tried to go for an unconcerned response. Greta gave her a sharp look but didn't say anything. She unwrapped the fabric, then unfolded it, tossing it across her knees.

"Dragons," she muttered and sighed. "I suppose we had to." Then she squinted closer. "Are they . . . playing tennis?" Her voice pitch made Tess wince. Not good.

"Yeah, I think so," Tess said, trying to convey the impression of someone who didn't know every single detail of the design perfectly, because it made no difference to her.

"That one's reading a book . . . we've got some gin rummy over here. . . ." Tess saw the smile creep across Greta's face. "This is really cute." The tension slipped

from Tess, to be replaced by a warm glow of gratifica-
tion. "Where did you say you got it?"

Tess blinked in surprise. Of course Greta would want
to know the name of the supplier. "Uh, that's from Custom Fabric Designs Unlimited." She flinched. Okay, it
was descriptive but it was also awful. But Greta was
nodding as if most suppliers sported descriptive but
awful names. "Where'd you find them?"

"Michael had some suggestions," Tess said, which
wasn't a completely bald-faced lie.

"Michael has a good eye," Greta said. "Custom designs? Can they really do custom fabric design?"

"Sure."

"That'd be great. I've been wanting to find a custom
fabric design shop that can do short print runs. All my
New York firms charge enough to make you faint, with a
five thousand yard minimum. Can they do wallpaper?"

"Don't see why not," Tess said. "Wallpaper?"

"Oh, yes. People always want paper to coordinate
with their fabric. There's always Waverly and other
companies like that but if you want something that isn't
traditional floral or stripes, you're out of luck. Around
here we get a lot of people who would rather live without furniture than do something traditional."

"Huh," Tess said. "I didn't realize you were looking
for a company like that."

Greta shrugged. "It's just something I've often felt
would help us expand what we do in the business."
Greta pulled the fabric closer, looking at it more intently.

She rubbed the panel between her fingers. "Pretty good quality."

"I'm sure they can upgrade the material to whatever you need. I told them we were looking for something very lightweight." Why was she carrying on the act? She should tell Greta now that she'd designed the piece. What was holding her back? They could share the excitement. But she resisted. This was hers and she wanted to enjoy it. She wanted to be the one in charge, not Greta.

"This is fine for those screens. What do they charge for exclusive fabrics? Is it a gazillion bucks a yard?" Greta asked. "You know Tina Lee would die if she could have a fabric that no one else would ever have."

"I don't know how much they charge," Tess said. "I suppose there would be a pretty hefty design fee since they couldn't reuse it, and then the setup and print-run costs. Do you want me to find out?"

"Yes. If they can come in at under three hundred dollars a yard, I can sell it to Ms. Lee in twelve seconds." Greta had her notebook out, her pen flying as she noted down her thoughts.

Three hundred dollars a yard, Tess thought, and had to sit down on the edge of the bed. A couple of hours to design a piece—be generous and say two full business days—plus the setup and print-run costs . . . she could clear a hundred dollars a yard. A hundred dollars a yard. Maybe more. Five yards would pay a month of Belinda's tuition. Fifty yards would pay for the entire year.

"I'll find out for you," Tess said, clearing her throat,

visions of dollar bills fading as she spoke. "What do you want to do about the Hendersons?"

Greta glanced up. "What? Sorry, I was just trying to think of some other projects that we could use custom fabric and paper designs for. A good half dozen right now. The price on that dragon fabric is a steal. Standard designer discount, right?"

"Right," Tess said.

"So we get a nice bit of change plus we'll look brilliant. Terrific stuff, great prices. Tess, this is going to make a big difference in how we set ourselves apart from the other interior designers in this town. Find out about their exclusive prices right away," she said. "And take that sample out to the Hendersons this afternoon. If they don't want it, I know some other clients who'd love it."

"Okay," Tess said. Her hands shook as she took the fabric and folded it. She wanted to tell Greta she was the one who had designed the piece so that she could hear Greta's compliments, but at the same time she didn't want Greta to know. It felt good to hear Greta's enthusiasm for the supplier when Greta had no reason to fake it, the way she would if she knew Tess was behind it all. And some small selfish part of Tess wanted to keep it to herself because if she didn't Greta would want to help . . . and Tess wanted this to be her own, her vision, her direction, even if she did fall flat on her face.

But she didn't seem to mind Michael helping, that irritating voice of reason in the back of her brain reminded her. That was different, she argued with the little voice. She and Michael had no history together. He was just investing in a business. Like a banker. Okay, also out of kindness, that was obvious. But he wouldn't have done it if he hadn't thought she was a good designer.

She called to make sure the Hendersons were home and agreed to meet them at their house after they both finished work. She said good-bye to Greta, who gave her an abstracted wave, busy with her brainstorming. She thought Greta was probably counting dollar bills too.

Chapter Eight

"Hey, Michael, do you have a minute?" Tess pushed through the double doors, juggling coffee cups as she went. She hadn't wanted to visit him twice on Friday—what if he misunderstood and explained about how he didn't date anyone and he liked her as a friend?—so she'd waited until Monday to report what the Hendersons had said. She'd looked forward to Monday morning like a teenager looking forward to a date. She could have called to tell him the news—that was what a prudent woman would have done—but she wanted to share it in person.

No matter how much she tried to tell herself to forget about it, that she was all wrong for him, that she couldn't fix him, that he wasn't ready or interested, her pulse still raced when she thought about him, the excitement still spread through her stomach. How pathetic was that?

"In here," Michael called from the finish room. She went in, handed him a cup. He was crating a chair for shipment.

"Thanks," he said, putting down his hammer and taking a grateful sip of coffee.

"The Hendersons loved the fabric."

"Of course they did. Was there ever a question?"

She rolled her eyes. "Of course there was. Tastes vary, you know."

"I know. But I never doubted you, Theresa," he said.

He was the only one who called her that. She liked the way it sounded when it came from him, warm and husky. It gave her the shivers. He could call her anything and she would like the way it sounded. "You over there," he could say, and it would make her shiver and her heart would thud happily in her chest. How pathetic was that?

So. She'd said what she came to say. She could send him a check for his share of the money when it came in. She didn't need to be here. *Off I go now,* she thought, not moving.

"Oh," he said, snapping his fingers. "You haven't seen the finished settee yet, have you?"

She had to focus to remember what he was talking about. Right. She'd made a cushion for the Weatherhill settee. Did she need to see the finished object? No. She could just say, "I'm sure it's fine, Michael," and go away. That would be sensible. Just say no. . . .

Michael put his cup down on the file cabinet and she followed suit, picking her way after him through the piles of furniture in various stages of finish. She wasn't going away. She was following the man like she had nothing better to do when in fact she had many better ways to spend her time. Productive ways. Ways that wouldn't leave her heart mangled by the side of the road.

"Don't you ever sleep?" she asked as she made her way through the welter of furniture. "You only have one helper, right? Plus Renee part-time in the showroom. How do you manage all this?"

Michael glanced over his shoulder at her, shrugged. "I don't have many distractions."

Ah. He had no life either. The knowledge made her feel obscurely better.

"Here it is," he said, turning a corner and pointing. The settee stood out even amid the jumbled environment, beautifully proportioned, elegantly finished. The cushion she'd made was harmonious and inviting. She ran her hand along the back of the settee. "This is gorgeous. And look at this finish. I can practically see my reflection."

"I hope so. I must have put ten layers of varnish on that piece, rubbing for hours between each layer."

"Hours?" She arched a brow.

"Many minutes, then," he said, and here came that slow smile. Now she had trouble thinking. She kept coming back because of the promise of the smile, but he didn't mean the promise. He probably didn't even know he was making it.

"It's lovely. At least this will look good in the Weatherhills' living room," she said. "I'll let Greta know it's ready."

"Jimmy can deliver it whenever it's convenient."

She nodded. Okay, she'd seen the settee. She'd told him her news. Now she just needed to say, "Have a nice day, Michael." But somehow she didn't want to leave just yet. Because what she'd really be saying was, "Have a nice life," and she hadn't quite worked herself up to that yet. Pathetic.

"Greta says that she can use a lot more custom fabric," she said, spinning out the time she could spend with him. "Which is great, but it makes me a little nervous."

"She doesn't know that you're doing the fabric?"

"No."

"You should tell her."

She hunched a shoulder. "I know. But . . . I want to make sure it's the designs she likes, not just that it's me doing the designing, you know?"

He nodded but she was pretty sure he didn't understand. She doubted that he'd ever owed anyone anything. That gratitude could become a habit, making relationships complicated.

"I don't want this to be another of her projects," she tried to explain. "Go to the grocery store, refinish the basement, make sure Tess' business succeeds. I want her to use the designs because they suit the purpose, not because I'm the one who made them."

"I get it," he said. "But you really don't understand

how talented you are. That's the problem. Greta wouldn't buy a design, even from you, if she didn't think it was good."

"See, that's where you're wrong," Tess said stubbornly. He didn't know Greta in her fairy godmother role. "She would."

Michael shook his head, just as stubborn. "Greta doesn't do things like that. If she didn't like your designs, she'd encourage you to get more training, or help you find someone who found them to their taste. Or she'd emphasize what your real talent was. She'd support your efforts, but she wouldn't pretend that she could use your designs if she couldn't. Or if she didn't want to."

"Huh," Tess said, thinking about this.

"Greta is a very sensible person," Michael said. He didn't have to sound so admiring. "And she doesn't take many risks. What she admires most about you is that you *do* take risks."

"Not anymore," Tess said positively. "I've sworn off risks."

Again his slow smile. "So that's why you're starting your own company? Because small business startups are completely risk free?"

Suddenly Tess' knees felt weak. "Wow," she said softly. "I guess that's what I am doing, starting my own company. Maybe it's not such a good idea after all."

"It's a great idea," Michael said. "You just need to believe in yourself a little more than you do." Unexpectedly, he reached forward and touched her face, tilting her chin so he could look into her eyes. Now her knees went weak for a different reason. Without thinking, she reached up and touched his shoulders for support. The T-shirt he wore was thin and taut over his muscles and her fingers gripped tighter. A startled light glowed in his eyes and apparently taking her action for encouragement, he lowered his mouth to hers.

Uh-oh, she thought, and then his lips were warm and gentle on hers, drawing the breath from her body. He drew her close into his embrace until all she could feel was his heat and the hard planes of his body. Even better than she'd dreamed. With a sigh, she yielded against him.

"Michael?" Dimly she heard the voice from across the room and she dropped her hands like a child caught in the act. Michael released her and stepped back. Feeling as if she'd been splashed with cold water, Tess shook herself and followed him as he walked around to the front of the room.

"Mother?" he said.

Tess saw the tall, elegant blond woman framed in the doorway to the finish room. The woman gave Michael a warm smile, which faltered when she caught sight of Tess.

"New employee?" she asked in a cool voice.

"Business partner," Michael said.

"Business partner?" Her voice rose an octave, her brow arched in disbelief.

"Yes."

"I see," the woman said, though she plainly did not.

"I'm Theresa Ferguson," Tess said, extending her hand. The woman hesitated, then took her hand and shook it, the action firm but brief. "Mrs. Manning."

"I have to run," Tess said, not meeting Michael's eyes. "Have a good day, you two." Then she fled.

Michael watched Theresa make her escape. She didn't waste a minute. After the door slammed shut behind her fleeing figure, he turned his attention to his mother. Well, he thought, contemplating her, if he could have run, that was what he would have done too.

His heart still slammed in his chest from the kiss. It had been a good kiss, a memorable one, but it had been just a start. A man didn't kiss a woman like Theresa and then stop and call it a day. No, the kiss was just an opening gambit. It was just . . . hello.

It was a good thing his mother had come in when she did. Because he wasn't ready for this, for a relationship that went beyond hello.

"Who was that?" his mother asked, her voice cold and judgmental as usual. He never needed a cold shower when his mother was around. Staying in the same room with her for a few minutes cooled him right down.

"Told you," Michael said, wondering if his mother had somehow seen him kissing Theresa. Given that it was his mother, she could probably sense things like that without having to see them.

His mother narrowed her eyes at him. "Unsuitable," she sniffed.

"You do that wrong," he said. "You always have. You're going to drive me into her arms if you disapprove of her."

"You're not ready for a woman like her."

"I'm not discussing this with you," Michael said. How could you be ready for a woman like Theresa? There wasn't a single thing you could do to prepare. So you either decided to step to the plate and see what happened or you just walked away, knowing you'd be plagued by a lifetime of "what if's if you did.

His mother's face softened as she looked at him. "I just don't want you to get hurt," she said. "Haven't you been hurt enough already?"

"Here or to go?" Kevin asked. It was Tuesday morning—two-fer-Tuesday—so the place was buzzing and Tess had had to wait in line for ten minutes to place her order.

"Here," she said. "I have a commission to work on."

"A design?" Kevin asked, fixing the espresso. "Cool."

"Here's hoping I don't screw it up."

"Tess, how many times do I have to tell you the negative self-talk will kill you? You need an affirmation. Repeat after me: 'I am a talented designer and will impress the client.' "

"I am a talented designer and will impress the client," she repeated obediently.

"Now I want you to say that twenty times."

"You know, at some coffee shops in this city, they just serve coffee," she remarked as Kevin heated the hot chocolate.

"Yeah, and that's why you're in here," Kevin said. "Notice how you took my advice about your hair."

"Yes, Kevin, I hang on your every word."

"Sensible girl. So how is the manhunt coming?"

"I'm not on a manhunt."

"You sure look like you're on the prowl." He regarded her. "Although maybe you can't help that."

"It's either a gift or a curse, I can't decide which."

He nodded. "So how's romance?"

"Recently I've fallen for a man still in love with his dead wife," she said. "Though he did kiss me just before his mother walked in."

"Something about what you just described makes me want to go ew."

"Yeah, there's something wrong with having to interrupt a kiss because the guy's mother just walked in. At our age, you know? I felt like I was in high school again."

"That's not all that's wrong with what you just described. How long has this man been widowed, Tess? It's not like you to move in on someone who's recently bereaved."

"I know I should be more—what—reverent? But she's been dead seven years. You'd think the memory would have faded a little, you know?"

"Maybe." Kevin shrugged and dumped the espresso

and hot chocolate into a tall glass. "We're all different. Sometimes you find the person who's just right for you. Not almost right or close enough, but just right. If you lost a love like that—" He shook his head. "Maybe you'd never get over it."

"Maybe." Never having experienced such a thing, she wouldn't know. How she felt about Michael—she wasn't prepared to dwell on that. There was no future with him, so she had to let go of her childish fantasies.

"What's his mother like?" Kevin asked.

"I couldn't really tell. She has that chilly blonde thing going, and I could practically feel her distaste for me oozing from her pores."

"Well, if she saw you kissing him—"

"Afraid that I'm going to steal her little boy? He's been married! He must be thirty-five or forty. How ridiculous."

"It wouldn't matter how old Belinda was, you wouldn't want her getting hurt," Kevin said reasonably.

"You have a point. Anyway, it doesn't matter. It's not going anywhere. He already told me so. Therefore my plan is to stay as far away from him as I can get."

"Hi, Kevin," a voice behind her said. "Hi, Theresa."

Tess closed her eyes. Then she turned around and said brightly, "Hi, Michael! How are you doing this morning?"

Tess spent the next week working on designs for her new company at Greta's request. Since Greta didn't know Tess was Custom Fabric Designs Unlimited, she had to do the design work around her usual job with Greta. She worked long hours at her kitchen table and felt suitably disciplined and grown-up in her devotion to her work. She studiously avoided La Prima Tazza so she wouldn't run into Michael. That was either very adult in its common sense or very childish in its avoidance, she couldn't tell which. By the following Tuesday, all of the effort had left her tired and drained.

"What's up, Tess?" Greta asked at lunchtime.

"What do you mean?" Tess asked, picking at her sandwich.

"You seem down. You've been sighing all morning as if the weight of the world is on your shoulders." She gave Tess a speculative glance. "There's nothing wrong with Belinda, is there?"

"Belinda is fine," Tess said. "I'm mostly just annoyed with myself. I'm trying to avoid trouble so I've been sticking close to home."

"What kind of trouble?" Greta asked sharply, and Tess had a sudden memory of their youthful conversations about every concern a teenage girl might have. Greta had always told Tess she could come to her with any problems since their parents weren't the kind of people you turned to in a crisis. But that had been a long time ago.

"Not that kind of trouble," Tess said.

"What kind of trouble do you think I'm thinking

about?" Greta asked, eyes narrowing. Then she shook herself. "Never mind. The question is, what kind of trouble are you talking about?"

"It's nothing."

"It's not nothing," Greta said. "It's a man, isn't it?" She put her sandwich down and looked intently at Tess. "Yes. Who— Oh, Tess. Not Michael. Didn't I warn you about Michael? Didn't I say you couldn't fix it?"

"Indeed you did. I'm not blaming you," Tess said. "This has nothing to do with you." Although it did in fact have everything to do with Greta, because she was the one who sent Tess into the lion's den in the first place. But Tess was pretty sure such a reminder would not be appreciated.

Greta passed a hand over her eyes. "Tess, you're not his type. And he is not ready for—"

"For what?"

"For any kind of meaningful relationship." And then, not unkindly, "He's definitely not ready for you."

"He kissed me," Tess said defiantly. Honestly, Greta was acting like Tess was irrationally embarked on a one-sided obsession with the man. It wasn't quite like that.

"He kissed you?" Greta asked, incredulous. As if Tess might have misunderstood what had happened. No, she distinctly remembered how Michael had pulled her into his arms and given her a passionate kiss. It wasn't the kind of affectionate smooch you might give your little sister. She hadn't made a mistake about *that*.

"What did I tell you, Tess?" Greta demanded, shoving her plate aside as if she had lost her appetite. "You just never listen."

"Thank you for understanding," Tess said, taking the pickle from her sister's plate and munching on it to demonstrate that she was fine and not likely to lose her appetite over a silly thing like a romantic entanglement that could only lead to heartache.

"I wish I'd never asked. Now I have to worry about you."

"You don't have to worry about me," Tess said.

"Someone has to worry about you. You never do."

Tess took a bite of her sandwich. "Other people have bosses who let them eat their lunch without chastising them about their love life."

"Other people listen to their sisters when their sisters say, 'Try not to get involved with unsuitable men who will break your heart.' "

"You never said all that to me," Tess said. "By the way, I've got some quotes for you on those custom designs."

"Now that was a smooth change of subject," Greta said, but she made no further mention of Michael.

On Wednesday morning, Tess gave up the struggle and returned to her favorite coffee shop, only to be disappointed when she saw no sign of Michael. But she was somehow not surprised when he called her that afternoon and said, "I have those screens roughed out. Do you want to come by and take a look, make sure every-thing is what you expected?"

Tess didn't respond immediately. Supervising the carpentry was really Greta's job, but she still wasn't able to get around very easily.

"Theresa?"

"Sure. I'll stop by this afternoon." *Please be wearing your shirt when I arrive*, she added mentally.

When she pushed open the double doors to the work-shop, she noticed two things: it was hotter than a fur-nace inside and Michael *was* wearing his shirt, which, despite her solemn protestations to herself, was a crush-ing disappointment.

"Over here on the sawhorses," he said when she walked in.

She strode over to the place he indicated. Purposeful, businesslike. She was representing Interiors, ensuring that a subcontractor was producing a product of accept-able quality. Yes, there were the screens. They looked like they were supposed to look, but Michael must have known that. "Very nice," she said, for lack of any other comment she could make.

Michael gave her a curious look that said, *Very nice?* What he did say aloud was, "Thank you." He hung back from her, hands thrust in his jeans' pockets, staring at the ground, as if he were trying to summon the courage to speak.

Oh, no, she thought. *He's going to apologize for the*

kiss. I'm not sure my ego can stand it. Then her cell phone rang and she grabbed it out of her bag, thankful for the interruption. Anything to forestall an awkward conversation about the most interesting event that had happened to her lately.

"Tess, school just called," Greta said without preamble. "Belle fell at recess and hurt herself. She may have broken her wrist." They didn't have school nurses at the Montessori school that Belinda attended, so the teachers tended to err on the side of caution. Tess reminded herself of that when the panic rose in her throat.

"I'm on my way," Tess said, forcing down the panic. "Call the school back and tell them I'll be there in ten minutes." She turned to leave, then tossed a quick explanation to Michael over her shoulder. "Belinda's been hurt. I have to go."

Tess drove quickly and impatiently through town, constantly reminding herself that getting into an auto accident on the way to pick up her injured daughter from school wouldn't solve anything. Fortunately, the weather was clear and the traffic light, so she was able to make good time across town.

Finally she pulled into the drive in front of the school. She abandoned the car there, not even parking it in a slot, barely remembering to pull the key from the ignition.

She raced inside and down the hallway to Belinda's classroom. Belinda was sitting quietly on Mrs. Phillips' lap. The teacher was sitting cross-legged on the floor, reading her a book. The other children were working quietly at various stations throughout the room. Tess took a deep, sustaining breath. She'd imagined blood everywhere, bones sticking out of skin, all the gory trauma parents live in constant fear of.

"There's Mama," Mrs. Phillips said to Belinda, giving Tess a smile. Tess felt too agitated to return the smile and dropped to her knees next to the teacher. "Hey, sweetie," Tess said, trying to sound calm so she wouldn't scare Belinda. She brushed a strand of hair from Belinda's forehead. She could see a red bruise there. Belinda had been crying, Tess could tell that from the red eyes and the tear stains on her cheeks, but she seemed calm now. "Where does it hurt? Did you bump your head?" Belinda nodded. She held out her arm. Her wrist was badly swollen.

"What happened?" Tess asked Mrs. Phillips.

"She fell off the swing at recess," the teacher said. "I think she was in a contest with Mary Ann about who could swing the highest."

Tess nodded, an unwilling grin tugging at her lips. It was such a normal kid thing to do.

"She can't really describe how she landed or what hurts," Mrs. Phillips continued. "You can see her wrist is swollen and the bruise on her forehead. She doesn't appear to have any pain or swelling in her knees or ankles, and she seemed to be walking fine. But given the obvious bumps and bruises, I think it would be best to get her evaluated."

"Punkin' pie, we're going to have to see the doctor," Tess said. "Can you walk to the car? You're a little too big for Mama to carry you."

"Walk," Belinda said, climbing out of Mrs. Phillips' lap and getting to her feet. Tess guided her to the car and helped her in, doing her best not to bump the tender wrist. She kissed Belinda on the cheek as she buckled her in, then used her cell phone to call the pediatrician, who promised to meet them at the emergency room of the local hospital so they could get X-rays taken immediately.

It took only a few minutes to drive to the hospital, but then there was a long, aggravating wait as the admissions clerk took Tess' insurance information. Then a nurse took Belinda's medical history and details of the current problem and patiently answered a good half-dozen questions from Belinda, ranging from what her name was to how soon Belinda would feel better. After that, they were left alone for a while, while Tess' stomach knotted painfully and Belinda reminded her every few minutes that everything hurt.

Finally, they were called into an examination room and Belinda's pediatrician, Dr. Mendez, breezed in, a broad smile on his thin, animated face. That smile did a lot to dispel Belinda's fears. *Wouldn't you know*, Tess thought. Her daughter was susceptible to male smiles too.

"Stickers?" Belinda asked, her tear-streaked face turned up to him.

"We can probably arrange that," he said, running his competent, professional fingers over Belinda's limbs. "I bet this hurts," he said, touching her swollen wrist. Tears filled her eyes and she nodded, biting her lip, putting on a brave face for him.

Tess explained what the teacher had told her about the accident. He nodded, making notes on the clipboard in his hand. Then he spoke rapidly to the nurse, who had joined them in the room, and ordered radiology tests.

"She's going to be fine," he finally told Tess, turning back to her, "but we need to take some X-rays." He glanced at Belinda. "We're going to take a picture of your wrist and one of your head," he told her. "Do you think you can hold still for that?"

Wide-eyed, she nodded, but Tess could see the panic-stricken look in her eyes.

"Mama will be there," Tess reassured her.

Soon the X-rays had been taken and they returned to the exam room. Tess sat in the uncomfortable visitor's chair—definitely an afterthought in the room—and Belinda climbed unceremoniously into her lap, even though she was practically as tall as Tess and a little too big for lap-sitting. Tess didn't protest, just held her daughter in her arms, trying not to jostle the hurt wrist.

"You're going to be okay, honey," Tess said. "I love you."

"This much," Belinda murmured.

"This much," Tess agreed.

After a while, Dr. Mendez returned, pulling up the rolling stool and smiling his broad smile. "Well, Belinda, it looks like you did a number on yourself!" Belinda glanced over at him but kept her head nestled in Tess' shoulder. Dr. Mendez gave Belinda a gentle pat on the back, then turned his attention to Tess. "She has a broken wrist. We'll have to put a cast on it. The skull X-ray was inconclusive. I'm concerned about a possible concussion, so I'd like her to stay overnight."

Tess nodded, relieved that it wasn't worse, worried that a concussion would be dangerous for Belinda, calculating, in some corner of her mind, insurance deductibles and co-payments, realizing with a rush of relief that she would be able to meet her commitments thanks to the fabric design work she was doing. *Thanks to Michael,* she thought, her heart squeezing. Because he'd believed in her.

Dr. Mendez was talking to the nurse again and ordering the materials needed to cast Belinda's arm.

"I'm going to call Aunt Greta and tell her the news," Tess said to Belinda. "I'll be back in a second, sweetie. I'm not supposed to use my cell phone in here."

"Be back?" Belinda asked.

"In one minute. Before you know it. I'll be right back."

Belinda looked unconvinced, but Tess gave her a hug, deposited her on the exam table, and headed outside where she could use the cell phone. The nurse was digging through drawers to find Belinda a sticker as Tess left the room.

Greta picked up on the first ring, which was not like her, but which showed how worried she was. "Belinda's going to be okay, but she broke her wrist," Tess said, not even bothering with niceties such as "Hello" and "How are you?" She wanted to get back to Belinda right away. "They're worried about a concussion so she'll be here overnight. I'll stay with her, so don't expect me tomorrow. We'll both be dead tired by morning."

"You don't actually think I care about work tomorrow," Greta said. "I'm just glad the little munchkin is going to be okay. I'll stop by—"

"You don't need to come out here. She'll be home tomorrow," Tess said.

She heard the sigh that showed Greta was exhibiting great and restrained patience. "As I was saying, I'll stop by later tonight. She's going to be bored and cranky by dinnertime," Greta predicted.

"I don't know how you can drive that stick shift with your knee out of commission."

"Huh," Greta said.

"I thought you might have forgotten about that," Tess said.

"I'll call a friend."

It never occurred to Tess that Greta, of all the friends she might have summoned, would call Michael. At least not until later that day when she saw his tall rangy figure a step or two behind Greta as Greta thumped into Belinda's hospital room on her one crutch.

For a moment, Tess thought about never speaking to

her sister again. Hadn't they just had a conversation about Michael? Hadn't Greta warned her to steer clear? Hadn't Tess had every intention of avoiding him as much as possible? Now Greta was dragging him into Tess' life again. Okay, not exactly dragging him into Tess' life again. She'd gotten a ride to the hospital from him. But still. Watching him looking calm and strong and competent, Tess wished she could have the comfort of his arms around her. She wouldn't feel so alone then. *Don't be silly,* she told herself. She had Greta. But somehow it wasn't quite the same.

"Hey, Belle," Greta said, ignoring the look Tess shot her. "I brought you something. A girl can't land in the hospital and not get a little something for her troubles."

"Present?" Belinda asked, perking up. "Brought me a present?"

"Sure did," Greta said. "I would have brought flowers but I suspected you would not appreciate the sentiment. Maybe when you're a little older."

"Present?" Belinda demanded.

Greta slung her bag off her shoulder and dug through it, pulling a paper sack from its depths.

"Belinda," Tess said. "What do you say?"

"Present?" Belinda asked.

"Belinda," Tess said, using her warning voice.

"Thank you, Aunt Greta," Belinda recited, grabbing the sack out of Greta's hands. Pulling it open, she thrust her good hand inside and pulled out a small stuffed tiger and a book of stickers. She shook the bag to make sure she'd gotten all the goodies, then shoved it aside. Tess dropped it in the wastebasket. Belinda tucked the tiger under the covers with her, leaving only its nose peeping out. "*Finding Nemo!*" she exclaimed, opening the sticker book. "Love *Finding Nemo!*"

"I thought you might," Greta said. "Can I sit next to you there? My knee hurts."

"This is my good side," Belinda said, patting the mattress. Greta leaned her crutch against the wall and sat on the bed where Belinda indicated. "Here's Nemo! Nemo is a clown fish. The blue fish is Dory."

"Is that right?" Greta said, rolling her eyes. "I would never have guessed."

"Michael, come on in," Tess finally said as he leaned against the doorjamb. "How did Greta rope you into driving her out here?"

Michael came into the room and took the visitor's chair next to Tess. "I called her to find out how Belinda was. Greta said she'd just gotten off the phone with you and was on her way over if she could find someone to drive her."

Greta gave her a glance across Belinda's bowed head. "Sorry," she mouthed. Tess shook her head. She knew Greta could easily have asked her friend Monica for a lift. So why had she turned to Michael? Well, what else could it be but a coincidence? Greta surely didn't have any ulterior motives.

"Brought me a present?" Belinda asked, looking up from her sticker book to fix her clear gaze on Michael.

"I brought you Greta," he said. "Does that count?"

"Belinda, don't be rude," Tess chided gently.

"What's rude?"

"Asking people if they brought you presents."

"Why?"

"Because we should appreciate having friends. They shouldn't have to bring us presents for us to look forward to seeing them."

Belinda pushed her hair out of her eyes and looked at Tess. How much of that explanation did she understand? Tess wondered, as she often did.

"Never mind," Greta said, kissing Belinda on the forehead. "I know the feeling. Presents are good."

"Presents are good," Belinda agreed readily. Then, "Look!" She thrust her hand toward Greta.

"That's some cast you've got there," Greta said. "Does your arm hurt very much?"

"Broked my wrist!" Belinda exclaimed. "Gave me a shot! Don't like shots."

"The pain shot will make you feel better soon," Greta said. "Why, I believe I'm going to be the first person to sign this here cast." She opened her bag and produced a blue felt-tip pen. She drew a cluster of hearts and signed her name on the cast.

"Mama, do that!" Belinda said excitedly. "And Michael. And everyone!"

"You bet," Tess said, taking the pen from Greta and sketching a tiny likeness of the tiger Greta had brought.

"Get well soon, tiger," she said as she wrote the words. "Love, Mama."

Belinda looked expectantly at Michael as he simply signed his name to the cast. "No hearts or cute animals for me. I'm not getting into a creativity contest with those two," he explained, handing the pen back to Greta.

"Okay," Belinda said, patting him on the cheek.

A clatter outside the door signaled the arrival of the dinner cart. A moment later the dietary aide swung through the door, carrying a tray.

"Looks like your supper is here," Tess said.

"Why don't you get something to eat?" Michael asked Tess. "Greta says you're planning to spend the night here. You might as well grab something now. We can sit with Belinda until you get back."

"Good idea," Greta said. "I need to catch up on my *Finding Nemo* facts anyway."

"You don't have to—"

"Oh, good heavens, don't argue," Greta said. "Go down to the cafeteria, get something to eat. Grab a magazine from the gift shop. It's going to be a long night for you."

"I'll come with you," Michael said as if all that was stopping her was the lack of a dining companion.

Of course, Tess thought. *That's all I need now.*

"I'm—" Tess began, then relented at the look on his face and didn't say the rest of the sentence—*capable of eating alone.* "Fine, come along," she said instead.

"What do you say, Mama?" Belinda asked.

"Thank you," Tess said to Michael. She ruffled Belinda's hair and said, "You're turning into a smart aleck."

"Smart aleck?" Belinda asked. But Tess decided to leave that for Greta to answer.

Chapter Nine

"**I** *am* hungry," Tess said. "Although I have to say the menu leaves a little something to be desired." Under the harsh fluorescent lighting, the choices in the hospital cafeteria looked even less appealing than they might have.

"Hospital food," Michael agreed. His voice was neutral but she snapped a look up at his face. She remembered that his wife had died in an auto accident. With horror, she realized that his wife might have lingered for a while before dying. A shudder ran through her body. Maybe that was why he hadn't been able to move beyond the tragedy. Maybe she'd been hospitalized for days. The agony of such an experience would be hard to heal from.

She picked up a salad, a roll, and a few pieces of

171

fruit, placing them on her tray. Michael grabbed a cup of coffee, saying he'd eat later, at home. She didn't blame him. She paid the cashier, carrying her food to a small table in the corner, where Michael joined her. He sipped at his coffee, making a face at the taste.

"Boiled?" Tess asked. "Or is it just that you've gotten used to having mocha?"

"Probably both," Michael said, putting the cup down. "That's the problem with indulgences. They stop being indulgences after a while and then when you go back to the regular thing, which is perfectly good, you feel disappointed."

"Now there's a depressing worldview," she said without thinking. "You must be related to my ex-husband."

Michael raised an eyebrow but didn't say anything despite the fact that her comment would have been sufficient to start an argument with most of the men she knew.

"Sorry," Tess muttered. "I'm tired."

"From what I gather, I wouldn't want to be like him," Michael said. But still, it was just a comment, not a gauntlet thrown down.

"Forget it," Tess said. "It wasn't even apt. He's more inclined to think you can never get enough indulgences, and that he's earned as many as he can possibly grab on to."

Michael took another sip of the coffee. "Does he live around here? Will he come to see Belinda?"

Tess chewed salad and thought about ignoring the

question. Because it required explanations and she wasn't in the mood for explanations. She was tired and she just wanted to eat her dinner. On the other hand, she'd asked him plenty of painful personal questions and he'd answered them. Turnabout and all.

"I could call him and let him know what happened," Michael offered. "Or if he needs transportation, I'd be happy to help."

"No," Tess said. "He won't be coming. He's not Belinda's father."

A shadow seemed to pass over Michael's face. "I see," he said, and she could hear the judgment in his voice.

If he's going to be like that, the voice in the back of her head said, *let him think what he wants.*

She studied him over the cup of coffee in her hands. To give him the benefit of the doubt, what else was he supposed to think? He'd naturally assumed Belinda was a child of her marriage. Anyone would think the same.

"I need a piece of pie," she said. "To fortify myself."

"You don't have to talk about it if you don't want to."

"I know," she said. "It's not that mysterious. It just requires—fortification. Hold tight, I'll be back in a second."

She returned with a slice of apple pie and two forks. She handed one of the forks to Michael and he looked at it and then at her for a moment. *Another indulgence,* she thought. *He doesn't know what to do.* "Go on," she urged. "We can share." He lifted the fork, then took a bite from the side closest to him.

"Not bad," he said.

"Not bad at all," Tess agreed. "Let's see if I can give you the abridged version of the story of Belinda's life. It started when my best friend from high school got pregnant. We were in our midtwenties then, so she probably should've known better. She was single at the time, and she was having some problems." *Problems* didn't quite express it. She sighed again and said, "Julia started drinking a lot in college and then got caught up with a group of friends who did drugs, and pretty soon she was doing them too. We'd drifted apart by then. At the time, I wasn't much smarter, married to a bad-boy musician who I thought just needed the love of a good woman to turn his life around. Greta tried to warn me, but she stood up for me at my wedding anyway."

"Greta is a good sort," Michael said.

"The best." She could feel Michael's eyes on her but she didn't look up. It was easier to tell the story without looking at him. To some people, the story reflected badly on Tess. She hoped he wasn't one of them.

"So my friend Julia had a habit of picking men who weren't good for her," she said, not adding *just like me*. "One of the losers knocked her up, then beat her up for getting pregnant. She didn't really have any family to help her. But there I was, married, good job, stable home life. Carl and I had our fights, but I wasn't going anywhere. And if there was a problem that needed fixing, I was your gal."

"Nothing wrong with helping people out," Michael said gently.

"Sure. But I never think ahead, you know? When Greta does something, she figures out the worst-case scenario and then if it comes around, she's prepared for it. Not me. I just wade in there thinking I'm solving problems and I usually end up creating more than there were before I got started."

"I somehow doubt it," he said. "But that's a conversation for another time. Then what happened?"

"Then Julia had the baby, who was born with fetal alcohol syndrome. I was with her at the time. I named Belinda, you know? She was mine from the beginning. Julia abandoned her in the hospital. Just left her there. I guess the need for a fix was stronger than anything else. So. I knew Belinda would end up in the foster care system. And maybe some good adoptive parents would come along, but she was a problem baby. She's biracial, with special needs."

"I don't know much about fetal alcohol syndrome," Michael said. "Does it lead to mental retardation?"

"It can," Tess said. "Even from the beginning, it was clear Belinda was going to need support all of her life. So it wasn't a good bet that she'd be adopted by anyone. But there I was, ready to solve the problem. I became her foster mother. My ex stuck it for a while but he just didn't have it in him." She set her fork down, suddenly sick at the memory. She'd spent so much time angry at her ex for his weaknesses and equally angry with herself for bringing in the problem that exposed those weaknesses. "He wanted more, you know? He didn't want to be stuck with this imperfect child. Tied down, having obligations. And with Belinda, the obligations weren't going to end when she turned eighteen. Carl was going to be a brilliant musician and we held him back. There was always something better just around the corner for him. A prettier woman or a record company contract. What he had was never enough."

"Some people are strong when they're confronted by challenges. Some people just fold," he said.

Tess nodded. "He was one who folded. He took it out on Belinda, like she didn't have enough problems. I put up with a lot from him but when he started being so mean to Belinda, I left him. He told me when I divorced him that he thought we'd still be married if not for her."

Michael covered her hand with his. "So you think if you hadn't solved the problem with Belinda, you might have saved your marriage? Is that what you mean by creating more problems than there were?"

"Something like that. I mean, it's okay when the choices you make affect only you. But that affected him too, you know? And it wasn't fair."

"Marriage isn't about what's fair," Michael said. "You're supposed to do the tough stuff together. What if a child the two of you had together was born with special needs? Do you really think he would have been a better father to that child?"

"I don't know," Tess said. "I never gave him that chance. I just made a decision and who cared what he thought?" She took a deep steadying breath. "But then how can I regret it? I have Belinda. She's the light of my life, you know? If the cost was my marriage, so be it. In all honesty, it wasn't such a good marriage anyway. But not long after I divorced him, I lost my job, and now I had a little girl to take care of. Then I—well, I trusted someone I shouldn't have, and ended up with my bank account cleaned out. So I had to come to Greta and ask for help. She was only a few years out of her own rocky marriage, trying to make a success of her business. And that was another thing. I made Belinda her problem."

"That's what families are for."

She gave a shaky smile. "That's what Greta says. But look what trying to fix a problem led to?"

"Believe me, I understand what you're saying," he said. "But I just can't see where you were wrong to do what you did."

"I can't either," she said honestly. "But it just . . . affected so many other people. I never expected that. My parents disapproved. They told me I was irresponsible and that someday I'd grow up and stop trying to save the world. They were especially vehement because of Belinda's problems. They wanted no part of that. It was the last straw for our relationship. Julia—my best friend ever—hated me for interfering and refused to let me adopt Belinda. She would have had to sign away her parental rights. But at the same time, she wouldn't even do the bare minimum needed to convince the social services people to give her custody. And she could have gotten it if she really wanted it. I would never have opposed it if she were clean and sober, even though it would have broken my heart to give Belinda up."

"What happened to Julia?"

"Drug overdose after the judge denied one of her petitions for custody of Belinda," she said slowly. She'd never stopped blaming herself for that. If only she could have gotten through to her friend. If only Julia hadn't hated her so much, accused her of taking away her baby. Tess knew logically that it wasn't her fault, that Julia had abandoned her newborn daughter, but she felt responsible all the same.

"That became your fault too," he guessed.

Tess didn't answer, but she knew she didn't need to. "I was finally able to adopt Belinda, which made me happy. But I feel like the world is littered with the fallout from my decision to fix the problem. I mean, she could have gone to a good home, right? Or maybe Julia would have gotten her act together if I hadn't interfered. I'm not omniscient; I don't know what would have happened."

"You did the best you could," he said, his voice still gentle. "And you did it because you have a good heart."

"You sound like Greta."

"Of course I sound like Greta. Greta is an intelligent, right-thinking individual."

She shook her head, not knowing what to say.

"You've got a great kid in Belinda," he said. "And you're doing a great job with her."

Tess swallowed hard, feeling a little tearful. The story was always hard to tell, and despite Michael's kind words, Tess knew she deserved some blame for what happened. "Thanks for—understanding. Now, I'm going to ask you another favor. Someone needs to let the dogs out."

"Dogs," he repeated. "Am I right in suspecting that these are strays you happened to pick up in the course of a colorful life?"

"Something like that," she admitted.

"No problem," he said.

Tess passed a restless night in the chair by Belinda's hospital bed, but it was no worse than poor Belinda's. The nurse came in frequently to rouse Belinda and check her vital signs. By breakfast time on Thursday, Belinda was fretful, cranky, and out of sorts, and Tess felt overwhelmed and unable to cope because of her own fatigue.

When the nurse came in to check Belinda's vital signs again, Tess splashed cold water on her face, ran fingers through her tangled hair, and went down to the cafeteria for a cup of coffee and a bagel, which she brought back to Belinda's room. By then, Belinda's breakfast had been served. The nurse gratefully yielded her place at Belinda's side to Tess. Belinda insisted that she couldn't feed herself because of her broken wrist.

Tess reminded her that she wasn't left-handed but helped her even so.

Later in the morning, Dr. Mendez arrived to examine Belinda, read her chart, and discuss how her night went with the nurse on duty. Satisfied that the little girl had sustained no injury more serious than the broken wrist, he wrote discharge instructions and reminded Tess to call if Belinda had any problems and to schedule a follow-up visit with his office.

Thankful to be out of the hospital, Tess bundled a fussy Belinda and her belongings into the car and brought her home. Knowing her daughter was still in a lot of pain and wouldn't want to be isolated in her bedroom, Tess made a cocoon for her on the sofa, drawing one of the side tables over so Belinda could reach a snack, a drink, and the sticker book Greta had given her. Tess tucked the small stuffed tiger under the covers with her. She shooed the dogs out of the room but Belinda didn't mind having Penelope, the Persian cat, curl up on the sofa with her.

Then Tess put *Finding Nemo* in to play while she took a quick shower. When she was finished, she listened for Belinda but didn't hear any sound except for the movie. She toweled her hair dry, then slipped into an old sweatsuit.

Coming out of the bedroom, she saw that Belinda had fallen sound asleep on the sofa, so she grabbed her sketchbook and pencil even though she wanted to take a nap too. Sitting in the chair by the window, she started to sketch. Silver lining, she thought, looking up and watching Belinda's chest rise and fall as she slumbered. Tess spent the morning working on her designs but when Belinda woke around lunchtime, she required every modicum of Tess' attention.

By early evening, Tess felt frazzled by Belinda's fretful, whiny demands. Just a few more hours, she reminded herself, and then it would be bedtime. But the hours weren't moving very quickly and she didn't expect that Belinda would sleep very well that night either.

"Want Aunt Greta," Belinda demanded later that afternoon while Tess was inspecting the cupboards to see what she could fix for dinner, wishing she hadn't put off grocery shopping again.

"Aunt Greta can't come over," Tess said. "She can't drive."

"Go get her," Belinda demanded, imperious.

"Sweetie, I can't leave you by yourself and I'm not going to drag you all over town just so you can see Aunt Greta. You need your rest."

"Want Aunt Greta," Belinda wailed.

"How about calling Aunt Greta on the phone?" Tess offered.

Belinda sat with her arms folded across her chest. She gave an experimental sniff to see if Tess would yield further.

"Yes or no," Tess said.

Belinda let a tear trickle down her face. Tess held firm, not easily. "Talk to Aunt Greta," Belinda finally surrendered.

Tess brought the phone over to her daughter. "Say the numbers," Belinda said, her fingers hovering over the dial. Tess recited the phone number and Belinda punched it in. Tess watched as Belinda listened and the phone rang in Greta's house. "It's a message," Belinda said, handing the phone back to Tess, disappointment vivid on her face.

"We'll try her again later," Tess said, smoothing a hand across Belinda's soft cheek, hoping to forestall the tantrum she sensed was coming on. She wondered where Greta could be.

A few minutes later, Tess heard a sharp knock on the front door. She hurried down the hall, guessing that it was Greta, smiling broadly when she realized she was correct.

"I thought it was probably my turn to bring supper," Greta said, limping into the room, moving under her own power without crutches. She waded through the dogs, who had come tearing back into the room at the sound of the front door opening. Tess scooped up Max, the marmalade cat, out of Greta's way.

"Okay," Tess said. Greta held a drink carrier but Tess saw no sign of the supper Greta alluded to.

"He's coming," Greta explained briefly, and Tess didn't have to ask to whom the pronoun referred.

"Scoot over, kiddo," Greta said, setting the drinks on the table near the sofa and lowering herself to sit next to Belinda.

"Brought a present?" Belinda asked, then with a guilty look at Tess added, "Please?"

"I brought supper," Greta said. "That's better than a present."

"McDonald's?" Belinda asked.

"Yes, it is," Michael said, coming through the front door, juggling a fistful of bags and shutting the door behind him with his elbow. The dogs leaped up to investigate but Tess called them back and sent them outside.

"Good," said Belinda, smiling her approval and reaching for food. "Here."

"Give him a chance," Tess said. Michael dropped the food on the table and Belinda dug in, coming up with a box of fries and smiling triumphantly, then settling back against the cushions to munch happily.

"Where's mine?" Greta asked, and Belinda found a box of fries for her, rewarding her with a bright smile.

Tess pulled two chairs around so they could all sit in a group around the sofa. "Thanks, you two," Tess said, unwrapping a sandwich. "Belinda was hoping to see you tonight, Greta." She didn't say anything about who might have been hoping to see Michael. But not wanting to sound ungracious, she turned to him and added, "I appreciate your helping Greta out so she could come see us, Michael."

"No problem," he said.

Of course.

Later, Michael and Tess cleared away the remains of the meal while Greta agreed to tuck Belinda into her bed, promising to read her a bedtime story. "Not *Find-*

ing Nemo," Greta said as Belinda led the way down the hall to her bedroom.

Tess grabbed the trash bag and headed out the front door. "Trash day tomorrow," she explained over her shoulder.

Michael ambled along after her. "Nice night out," he said, propping his hip on the porch rail. Despite the darkness, the evening air was still warm with spring. Tess tossed the bag into the trash can and dragged the can to the curb. Then she joined Michael on the porch rail.

"I need some lawn furniture," she said, wriggling to find a comfortable position. "I always seem to have more month than money. It doesn't seem right to stick those cheap plastic chairs from Wal-Mart out here."

"You've gone to a lot of work," he remarked.

Tess looked at the flowers. "Belinda likes to help me garden and I'm partial to flowers," she said. "Not really interested in a lawn or a vegetable garden or anything. Just the flowers. Every spring those daffodils come up and it makes me happy to see them. No matter what kind of day it's been." Crocuses and tulips were also up but the daffodils delighted her the most.

"I enjoy gardens—and I even like gardening—but I don't make the time to do it myself," he said.

"I never did either when it was just me. Somehow it makes a difference having Belinda." Tess winced and wished she'd phrased the thought a little differently. She changed the subject. "I really do appreciate your bringing Greta by tonight," she said. "Whenever Belinda feels anxious, she likes to have the people she loves around her."

"Smart kid."

She took a deep breath of the warm evening air. The sun had set but she could see his smile by the glow of the porch light. "Hey, you'll be interested to know that Custom Fabric Designs just got two more commissions," she said.

"I'm not surprised," he said. A moment's hesitation, and then he added, "You need to tell Greta."

"I will," she said. "Soon. I swear. Oh, I'll have the fabric for the Henderson screens for you in a day or two. I should be able to get a check to you sometime next week." There, just business. No need to let him know she could feel his nearness in the dark, that if she leaned slightly to the right, she would brush against him. She caught her breath and took herself firmly in hand.

"Ah, the old check is in the mail ploy," he said, and she had to glance at his face to see that he was teasing. "I told you this whole project was risk free for me."

"You didn't know that at the time."

"Yes, I did."

His complacent tone was meant to rile her, she knew, so she ignored it. She shook her head and said, "You're as bad as Greta."

"At least you're not comparing me to your ex-husband," he said. "I don't mind being compared to Greta."

Tess managed a smile at his light, teasing tone but inwardly she sighed. Greta was a terrific person, but did he have to constantly say so? Obviously she was just his type. Why had he turned her down? Greta claimed he had courteously rejected her years ago—probably because he still hadn't gotten over losing his wife. But if he ever did, no doubt it would be Greta he wanted.

"Tell me about your wife," Tess said, her brain doing its usual free association and her mouth not closing in time. She wished she'd shut up. Couldn't she ever leave well enough alone?

"My wife?" Michael repeated although Tess knew he'd heard perfectly well. But she realized it would have seemed like a non sequitur to him.

"I told you all my past history," Tess said. "And I'm curious. I just, uh, you said that you don't date, and—" She stopped, wanting to writhe in embarrassment. Why had she brought this up?

"And you thought the two things might be related?" Michael asked. By the light of the porch lamp, it looked as if he might be trying to smile, though the effort was unsuccessful.

"Aren't they?" Tess asked. She already knew the answer; of course they were related. If only there was some way to make him see that he was entitled to a future. If only he were willing to take a risk. *I'm right here,* she wanted to say, but she didn't, she wouldn't. She got as close as she dared, pushing him on the personal questions. He must know why but he never gave her any indication that he looked at her and thought, *so that's my future.*

Michael considered her for a moment. "You always get right to the center of things, don't you?" he said.

She shrugged with a nonchalance she did not feel. "If you mean I'm not afraid to ask questions that aren't any of my business, yeah, I'm pretty good at that."

"Why do you want to know?"

Tess looked up at him. *Why?* If she had to explain that . . . "Never mind, Michael," she said.

"I'm sorry," he said. He reached out and touched her face. "You have a reason for asking or you wouldn't ask. The answer is yes, the two things are related."

Great, Tess thought, a film of unhappiness blanketing her heart. *I just love it when I'm right.*

"You're so different from her," he said. She could feel the warmth of his fingers still on her cheek. And he was so near, bending close. She ached for him, wanting to feel his lips on hers, his arms around her, pulling her to him. Then he dropped his hand and turned as Greta came onto the porch.

Tess brought her hand to her face where he'd touched her, then realized how the action betrayed her. Well, actually, asking about his late wife and his dating habits had probably given her away first.

"Am I interrupting something?" Greta asked, arching a knowing brow.

"No," Tess said.

"No problem," said Michael.

No problem, he thought, wanting to shake Greta. *Why couldn't I just tell her we were having a private conversation and she could go away now?* So he wasn't feeling very friendly toward her as he drove her home. If his seething silence bothered her—if she even noticed it—she didn't let on.

He'd been this close to taking Theresa in his arms and kissing her again. She would have let him. She revealed herself in a hundred different ways. Like with that dry "never mind." She tried not to be vulnerable, he could see that, but she wasn't very good at erecting barriers. What was worse, though, was that she made *him* feel unprotected, his innermost thoughts and feelings laid open to her. She kept cracking his barriers and slipping past. Never pulling them down but just . . . getting in anyway. Sliding under his guard. And then he wanted to kiss her and—and give the blessed woman some real furniture.

He could see that she'd done her best with limited means but the result shouldn't have made her seem so . . . *brave.* Despite difficulties, she was making a good home for Belinda with a little money and a little effort and a lot of imagination. Making a family out of a few good-hearted souls and assorted mammals.

He pictured daffodils, rioting everywhere. Hadn't the woman ever heard of a flower bed? Just flowers everywhere and a path to a fenced-in patch of dirt for the dogs to play in.

He had a very nice house himself and it was filled with grown-up furniture and the lawn was meticulously maintained. But he hadn't wanted to come back here.

His mother was curled up on the sofa with a book of poetry when he came in. It had been the same way all his life. Other people's parents had watched Johnny Carson or Jay Leno, but not his.

He dropped a kiss on her cheek and she gave him a smile. "Nice evening?" she asked.

It wasn't what she said, it was how she said it.

"Very nice," he said.

"You don't look very happy," she remarked, setting the book aside.

"Good night, Mother."

Just as well he hadn't stayed. His mother would have known, which wasn't a piece of ammunition he wanted her to have.

You're not ready for a woman like her, his mother had said. She was right. He wasn't ready for a relationship with anyone, but especially not with Theresa. Those direct, cut-to-the-chase questions took his breath away. He finally understood what Greta meant about her sister's take-no-prisoners attitude. When she wanted to know something, she found out. And if he didn't stop with her right now, she would find out everything. And he wasn't ready for anyone, least of all Theresa, to know the truth.

Chapter Ten

Belinda was able to go to school on Monday, a situation for which Tess was devoutly grateful. She loved spending time with Belinda, but the little girl had been fussy and uncooperative since she'd broken her wrist, demanding Tess' complete and undivided attention, despite Tess' needing to spend a little time on projects for work. All in all, it was frustrating and annoying for both of them.

So Tess was a little more cheerful than usual dropping Belinda off at school that morning. The children clustered around her, oohing and aahing at her cast—nothing Belinda liked better than being the center of attention, so that was a plus—and she happily invited them to sign her cast, pointing out where her mother and Aunt Greta and Uncle Michael had already signed it.

Tess' heart pinched when Belinda said "Uncle Michael." Where had she gotten that?

Making sure that Mrs. Phillips had her cell phone number in case she needed to be reached, Tess headed over to Greta's house for a morning session of catch-up.

Greta was at her command center, the big bed littered with folders and her drafting tools. She was staring at the laptop when Tess walked in. She barely glanced up to take the cup of coffee Tess handed her.

Tess dropped her bag on the bed and sat next to Greta, glancing over her shoulder at the computer screen. Greta was working on her follow-up schedule. She was getting around more easily and would soon be ready for site visits again.

"Where are we with the Blackhorse proposal?" she asked.

"I talked to Anita last week," Tess said. "Monday, I think. She wanted to show the preliminary design ideas to her mother and then set a budget."

"All right. I'll put her down for a phone call later in the week. She's another one who might be interested in custom fabric. She's aiming for a very specific ethnic look." Greta looked pleased, and Tess was happy that her work could help Greta do a better job for her clients. She quelled the feeling of guilt welling in her heart. She knew she needed to tell Greta the truth but now that Greta was giving her commissions—or at least, giving commissions to Custom Fabric Designs—she was finding it hard to broach the topic. She wished she'd been honest from the start. She'd do it, though. Just not right this minute.

"What else have we got going on?"

"The Henderson fabric came in," Tess said. "I can drop it by Michael's. I know he had the screens roughed out last week so I'm sure he's ready for it."

"I can always count on him," Greta said.

"Mmm," Tess said, forcing the beast of jealousy into a dungeon in her mind and slamming the door closed. The two of them made such a mutual admiration society, she didn't know why they weren't a couple. "I might as well do it now," she said, grabbing her keys and heading out the door.

A few minutes later, she squared her shoulders, climbed out of the car, dragged the fabric out of the trunk and marched into Michael's shop. Renee was at the front desk.

"I've got the fabric for the screens Michael's doing," Tess said, heading toward the double doors in back.

"He's not in," Renee said. "If you want to leave that here, I'll make sure he gets it."

Tess tried not to let her disappointment show. "Thanks," she said, placing the package on the desk. "It's for the Henderson project," she said. Renee made a note and smiled at her. "Anything else?" she asked when Tess just stood there.

"Uh, no. No thanks," Tess said, squashing the desire to ask when Michael would return so that she could invent another errand that would bring her back to his shop.

She needed to worry about those serial killers in her future since she couldn't seem to get over her compulsion to save the world. With a sigh, she knew it wasn't the world she wanted to save. Just one gorgeous carpenter with sad brown eyes.

"Tess?" Greta's voice sounded grim as Tess closed the front door. "That you? You want to come up here?"

Uh-oh, Tess thought. *What've I screwed up now?* Like a kid on the way to the principal's office, she trudged up the stairs, frantically trying to think what she might have done to put that tone in Greta's voice.

When Tess walked into the bedroom, she saw that Greta had a sketchbook in hand. Tess' brows drew together. That was her sketchbook. Then she spotted her bag on the bed next to Greta's knee and thought *uh-oh* again.

"I got a phone call," Greta said. "And I needed to take some notes and I couldn't find my pen." She gestured toward the disorder on the bed. "So I grabbed your bag and dug out a pen and a pad of paper. This pad of paper. I guess I should preface this by saying I'm sorry for looking at your stuff. I didn't mean to invade your privacy. But what is this?" She proffered the sketchbook.

"That's my sketchbook," Tess said, her heart hammering.

Greta turned to the page with the dragons on it. "Look familiar?" she asked icily.

"Oh. That." She bit back the queasiness in her stomach. She should have told Greta at the beginning. Why hadn't she?

"Yes. That." Greta's voice was cutting. Sudden tears welled in Tess' eyes, like a child caught misbehaving, being chastised by her mother. She hated having Greta mad at her. She knew exactly how Belinda felt when she got a scolding.

"You're Custom Fabric Designs Unlimited, aren't you?"

"Yes," Tess admitted, not able to meet her sister's eyes.

"Tess, why didn't you tell me? Why did you lie to me?"

"I'm so sorry, Greta. It's just—"

"Just what, Tess? What did you think I'd do if you told me you wanted to design fabric? Did you think I'd laugh at you? You know me better than that."

"It wasn't that," Tess protested.

"What was it?"

"I just—I wanted you to like the designs on their own merits. Not because I'm your sister."

"You think I would have been that patronizing?" Greta demanded.

"I don't know," Tess said miserably. "Wouldn't you? You've always supported everything I've done. But I've never known if it was because I'm good at what I do or if it's because I'm your sister."

"Huh," Greta said.

"I didn't mean anything by it. I just wanted your independent judgment."

"The problem is, this puts me in an extremely awkward position," Greta said. "Since you're a partner in Interiors, I should have disclosed to my clients that you also own Custom Fabric Designs. You see how my clients could look at it? They'd wonder what kind of conflict of interest might be going on, if I'm getting kickbacks for recommending your designs. I've always given my clients full disclosure and I've worked very hard to establish a reputation as a businessperson of integrity. Something like this casts doubt on my credibility."

"Oh, Greta," Tess gasped, her hand flying to her mouth. "That never occurred to me. I'm so sorry! It just never . . . I just never thought it through." Of course. She never thought anything through. "I'm so sorry," she whispered. The tears threatened to spill over. She turned to leave—

No more running away, she told herself. She had been doing that for too long now. She didn't meet Greta's eyes but stared at the sketchbook in her sister's hands.

She should have shown Greta the designs, asked for her honest opinion, and then brainstormed ways to make the company successful. Whether she liked the designs or not, Greta would have been happy to help. She might not have used them but she would have supported Tess' efforts. Besides, it wasn't up to Greta to decide if Tess were talented or if Tess could be successful. If Tess had really wanted to be independent in her success, she wouldn't have relied on Greta to sell the designs to her clients in the first place. After all, how was that being independently successful? Tess should have found her own clients if independence was that important.

No. If Tess was honest, it came down to this: she hadn't trusted herself or believed in herself. She hadn't wanted to share. Even worse, she'd liked Greta not knowing. Because she was just so tired of being grateful all the time.

That wasn't fair to Greta. Greta had never asked for gratitude. Greta just wanted them to be sisters who loved each other and helped each other out. Was Greta overcome with gratitude to Tess for helping her after her knee surgery? Of course not. She appreciated it, but she didn't think less of herself for needing help just because she'd hurt her knee.

I need to grow up, Tess thought. *I need to start seeing things the way they are. How can I expect other people to believe in me if I can't even believe in myself? I need to stop acting on impulse. I need to think things through.*

"I'm sorry," she said again.

"You should be."

Tess sat on the edge of the bed cautiously. "I just—I wanted something of my own, you know. Something that I didn't have to be grateful to you for."

Greta's jaw tightened. She knew her sister was trying very hard not to lose her temper. How many times had Greta tried to tell her she didn't need or want Tess' gratitude?

"I'll do whatever I need to do to fix it," Tess said. "I'll personally apologize to everyone. And maybe we can offer a discount on what they've purchased, or offer their money back. I'll be responsible for that."

"All right," Greta said. "Now tell me what I'm going to do with the Perdues."

Could it really be that simple? Could her sister really forgive the mistake and move on so readily? She looked at Greta's profile. Of course she could. Greta loved her. Tess wanted to hug her but wisely refrained.

"The Perdues," she said. "Hmm. Suggest marital counseling? Oooh, I know. Tell them that you think Alison Scott Designs would do a much better job for them. Cheaper too."

"That would be so cruel to Alison. I love it." Greta tapped a pencil against her teeth. "I could just start charging them by the hour."

"That's what I'd do," Tess said. "They'll never finish the house. They'll never even finish the living room, but you could pay your mortgage just listening to them disagree."

"I'll tell them that their budget is smaller than what I usually work with but that if they pay me by the hour . . . I can put up with a lot if I'm billing for every minute I stand there listening to them."

"There you go," Tess said. "Where are we with the Hendersons? Anything else I need to do?"

"Michael is going to install the screens later this week. I've got paper hangers coming in on Monday."

"I hope it all works out the way we were thinking it would."

"I'm never wrong about a design," Greta said.

"What about the Dzialowskis?" Tess asked.

"Don't push it," Greta said. "I've just barely forgiven you as it is."

On Wednesday morning, Tess planned to bring the check for his share of the fabric design income to Michael personally. Despite feeling bad about misleading Greta, she was pleased that the fabric design project was working out so well. Now she could repay Michael's investment with interest. Then . . . then what? Then they would no longer be business partners. She wouldn't need to keep seeing him. That was a good thing. Or so she told herself.

She stopped by La Prima Tazza for two mochas and drove to Michael's shop. She saw the clouds growing darker overhead and hoped she could get her errands done before a thunderstorm started. Early May was notorious for bringing monsoonlike rains to Kansas. Of course her umbrella was hanging in the hall closet at home.

Renee was not at the front desk when Tess arrived, so she walked directly to the back. Pushing through the double doors to the workshop, she saw the door to the office ajar and the light on. She walked over and stepped into the office. In surprise, she saw Mrs. Manning sitting at the desk. The blond-haired woman looked up at her. The expression that crossed her face was not welcoming.

What did I do to you? Tess wondered. "Hi," she managed, sitting down quickly in the guest chair because her knees were shaking. *After all these years of Greta, you'd think I could handle a chilly, elegant blonde.*

"Hello," Mrs. Manning said.

"I came by to give Michael a check," Tess said, though why she felt she needed to explain anything to this woman was beyond her.

"He and James had to make a delivery. They should be back in about half an hour." The words were perfectly polite but to Tess they held a warning: *Begone, never to return! I will protect my child from you with my last breath!*

Tess looked at Mrs. Manning. She supposed the woman wasn't lying and that Michael and James—that'd be Jimmy—were on a delivery and would be back in the half hour she'd indicated. Tess didn't have half an hour to spend waiting for Michael to return. Especially not with the chilly blonde in the room. "I brought his coffee," she said. "Would you like it?" she asked, not needing two cups for herself.

"You bring him coffee?" Mrs. Manning asked, taking the cup and sniffing it as if it might contain rotten eggs. "Mocha? He drinks mocha coffee?"

"He does now," Tess said with a grin.

Mrs. Manning took a gulp of the coffee, apparently to steady her nerves, though why her nerves would need steadying was beyond Tess. She seemed cool and calm. Disciplined. Efficient. *That's where he gets it from,* Tess thought.

She debated whether to just leave the check for Michael. She could jot a note and leave it on his desk. Then she would be done. Her glance fell on a remnant of the dragon fabric he'd tossed on the desk. "Oh!" she said. "He's put the fabric in the screens. I want to look at them."

She jumped to her feet and headed over to the finish room. She wasn't surprised to notice Mrs. Manning trailing behind her. Afraid Tess would make off with a dining room table, no doubt. Tess opened the door and immediately saw the screens stacked on sawhorses, the panels waiting to be joined together and installed.

"Look at that," she breathed. The screens looked like works of art. "He is just so brilliant at his work. Would you mind lifting that end? I want to see this in the light."

Mrs. Manning gave her a doubtful look.

"I designed the fabric," Tess explained. "I want to see what it looks like in the light." Mrs. Manning nodded without speaking and helped her lift one of the panels off the sawhorses. Tess brought it into the workshop, propping it against one of the metal racks so the light could filter through the fabric.

"Look at that," she said. "This is going to be beautiful when it's finished and installed." A smile tugged her lips. She'd done something good. She'd pissed Greta off in the process, but there was no denying she'd made something good.

"You designed this fabric?" Mrs. Manning asked.

"Yes, I did." The words came out proud and confident.

"It's certainly . . . unusual," Mrs. Manning said. "Is that dragon reading a book?"

"Yes. And this one is swimming. These two are playing cards."

Mrs. Manning stared at the fabric for a long time. "Michael used to have just such a whimsical streak," she said finally.

"I know," Tess said. "He did that Noah's Ark."

"You've seen the Noah's Ark."

"Oh, yes. He gave it to my daughter."

"He gave the ark to your daughter?" Mrs. Manning said, and seemed to wobble a little. Then she caught her breath and asked, "What did you say your name was?"

"Theresa. Most people call me Tess." Michael didn't, as if using her formal name could keep things formal between them.

"Theresa," Mrs. Manning said.

Apparently his mother wasn't going to go with the nickname either.

"Theresa," she said again. "You're not his type at all."

"Right," Tess said. There were enough members of the you're-not-Michael's-type club to form a support group. "Don't worry, I'm not going to hurt him."

"Oh, I'm sure it's much too late for that," Mrs. Manning said.

Tess had forgotten to leave the check. She knew she could simply put it in the mail, but she wanted to deliver it personally and thank him for believing in her and her project. And then . . . then Greta could deal with him from here on out. She'd understand—and so would he.

The next morning, she squared her shoulders to try again. Renee wasn't at the front desk when she came in, so she walked back to the double doors and pushed her way through to the workshop as she'd done so many times before. She wondered if this might be the last time. Her heart sank a little. She'd liked it here. She'd even liked Jimmy and the smell of sawdust and the whine of power saws. She wouldn't have thought it was her element at all, but she liked it. She especially liked the feeling that she could walk in here without an invitation. She'd miss it. She'd miss the tall, rangy man, strong and calm and competent, stuck in a past that would never give him love or laughter or—or children. How could you stop a fool from being a fool? A riddle for the ages.

She saw him at one of the workstations. The workshop was hot again and he had his shirt off. He was turning a table leg at one of the saws, his face intent as he worked, absorbed by what he was doing. The muscles in his back flexed as he moved and she wanted to touch him, to feel the warm skin under her fingers.

As if he sensed that she'd walked into the room, he looked up and he gave her that same slow smile. And her heart gave that same treacherous lurch. When he shut off the saw, she realized he was listening to George Strait on the stereo.

"Didn't figure you for a George Strait fan," she said.

He didn't seem to think her choice of subject matter was odd. "Jimmy just left on a delivery," he said. "Mondays, Wednesdays, and Fridays we listen to my music."

It was Thursday. Tess nodded.

"Isn't this what you were listening to when you taught him how to two-step?" he asked.

"Yes, we were listening to George Strait," she said, and she was finding it hard to breath, hard to concentrate on the words he was saying with him standing like that in front of her. Then she found her voice and said, "Shall I show you how to two-step?" She was moving closer to him. She should be moving farther away from him, that much was clear from the alarms clanging deep in her mind, but nope, she wasn't moving away from him. She was thinking this was her last chance to make a fool see reason. She wasn't sure if the fool was him or her. When she was through, one of them would see.

"I already know how to two-step."

"Of course," she said, stopping.

Then he took a step toward her. "I think you said . . . you start out here and who knows where you'll end up?"

"I say many things," Tess responded faintly.

Then his hand was on her waist and he was guiding her through the dance. She moved closer and then she closed her eyes and slid her arms around his neck. George moved into "Amarillo by Morning," and Tess knew she was lost.

She tilted her mouth up to meet Michael's but then he stepped back and released her.

"Theresa," he said, his voice hoarse.

"You know," she said, folding her arms across her chest, "for a minute there I was thinking you weren't going to say this to me."

"Say what to you?" he asked.

"You know: 'Tess, you're very sweet and attractive but you're just not my type. I'm not ready for this. I'm still not over my wife.' That."

He touched her face with infinite tenderness. "If I were . . . it would be you, Theresa."

"Lucky me," she said, and left the room.

Chapter Eleven

When Tess got home, she realized she still hadn't given Michael the check she owed him. It was the only thing that made her smile the whole weekend. All of that pain and she'd forgotten to do what she'd gone there for in the first place. She addressed an envelope and stuck the check in the mail. Then she watched *Finding Nemo* with Belinda. Four times.

Afterward, she broke out her secret stash of chocolate and ate it all. Then she treated them both to McDonald's for supper and still Sunday would not end so she could throw herself and her heartache into her work.

Which was probably just as well, she thought darkly, because Greta was sure to notice that something was wrong, and Greta was smart enough to recognize that two plus two in general led to four. Then Greta would oh so carefully refrain from saying, "I told you so." Tess would want to throw things.

Maybe she would call in sick on Monday. But then she would have all those hours to fill somehow, and the way things were going she would fill them with thinking about Michael and wanting to smack him over the head. *You're allowed to get on with your life,* she wanted to tell him. *You're allowed to move on to the next stage. You're allowed to make different plans.*

What is wrong with me? she wondered. But she knew. She was in love with Michael, who was in love with his dead wife, and how could you compete with someone who would never change, never grow old, never gain twenty pounds in her hips, never argue over whose turn it was to do the dishes? The beautiful blond dead wife would always be perfect and unchanging, caught in that moment of time when he lost her and his entire future.

The thunder boomed, startling Tess as she sketched at one of the small tables at La Prima Tazza. She glanced out the window and saw that the rain hadn't started yet, but the day had definitely grown darker and the air had become humid and clammy. It was going to be quite a storm. She turned back to her work.

Tess knew she was running a risk doing her work at the coffee shop, but she wasn't going to give up her favorite workspace on the off chance that she would run into Michael. If she saw him, she could give him a polite, freezingly cold hello—she'd learned that from Greta—and then ignore him. She hadn't seen him in the two weeks since he'd given her that tender brush-off.

But that morning, she hadn't even steeled herself against his potential arrival, and there he was, striding in the front door as lightning zigzagged across the sky and thunder crashed. She knew he spotted her at the table in the corner but he didn't even break his stride. He nodded at her, and she gave him a distant nod back, then turned her attention back to her sketchbook. Her current design was very absorbing. It required her complete, undivided attention. She didn't look up, didn't pay him any attention at all while he was telling Kevin what he wanted, while he paid for the coffee, picked up the cup . . . now he'd walk out the door. It hadn't started raining yet, but it would, so he should hurry. Except it wasn't her problem.

And he wasn't walking out the door. He was taking the chair opposite hers.

"Mind if I sit here?"

"I'm kinda busy."

"I can see that," he responded in such a gentle tone of voice that she felt ridiculous.

She looked up. "Hello, Michael," she said with careful patience. "I don't want to be your friend, thanks for the offer."

"I'm sorry," he said. "I know I acted as if I was interested in you—"

"You didn't *act* as if you were interested in me," Tess

said impatiently. "You *were* interested in me. I was there when you were kissing me, okay? We get along great, you're sweet to my kid, we're obviously interested in each other, but nope, that's not enough. You're not ready for a relationship. You know, at first I thought it was just that your wife was so perfect, how could I compete with that? You were so in love with her you'd never love another woman." She shook her head. "But then I realized I was wrong. Because ordinary human hearts heal. You never forget, you can never be the same, but you heal. And you, Michael, you have an ordinary human heart. You're just a man. And if you really did love her that much, eventually, one day you'd say, 'I want to try again.' Because when love is good, naturally you want more good love."

She dragged her hand through her hair. "You know how I figured that out? After I made Greta so mad and she forgave me. I knew she would. She loves me unconditionally. If I lost Greta, I would never be the same. But you know what? One day I'd want to find another person who loved me unconditionally. A friend I would love the same way. Because Greta has shown me what that means. I could never replace her but I would never dismiss the lesson she taught me. I know the love my sister and I have for each other is different from the love a man and a woman feel. But the lesson is the same."

She exhaled, studying him across the table. She wasn't getting through, she could tell that. He just gave her a calm look and sipped his coffee. The fool. She took a deep breath. She had nothing to lose. "What did your wife do to you, Michael?" she demanded. "Whatever it was went deep. And then she died and you could never dig it out. What was it, Michael? What did she do to you that destroyed your belief that you could ever be happy again? That you weren't entitled to be happy again?"

Michael's jaw had gone tense as she spoke, his face remote and angry at the same time. She had never seen him angry. For a moment she thought he was going to shout at her. Then he slammed his chair back and stalked out of the coffee shop. The thunder rolled, nicely in counterpoint. It started to rain.

Kevin glanced up at her from the table he was bussing. He raised his eyebrows at her.

"I handled that well," she said.

"What happened with you and Michael?" Greta asked later that afternoon. The worst of the storm had passed but Tess could still hear rain rattling against the window. "I was calling him about a project and he said he wouldn't be able to work on it until he calmed down."

"I ran into him at the coffee shop," Tess said. "And I told him I didn't want to be his friend. Then I said something about his late wife."

"That would explain it," Greta said. "You're always the soul of tact and diplomacy. Dare I ask what you said about his late wife?"

"I suggested she was less than perfect."

"You couldn't leave it alone?"

"When have I ever?" Tess said and felt the tears prick at her eyes. She dashed them away. "I never think. I just speak. It's a good thing I didn't want to be friends because I doubt he'll ever want to talk to me again."

Greta studied her for a moment before she responded. "Marianne at the Humane Society called for you." To someone else, it might have sounded like a non sequitur, but Tess knew better.

"Don't do this," Tess said.

"They've got an old blue heeler someone abandoned in the country that they haven't adopted out. Her number's up tomorrow."

"I don't have any more room."

"The city allows up to four dogs per residence without a license. So Marianne says, anyway."

"I don't do that anymore. I saw how it all ends, Greta. It ends with me proposing to a serial killer on death row, and that's not really what I want for my future. I've made a vow: no more fixing problems and no more taking in strays."

"Just checking," Greta said. "I'm glad to hear it. I think life will be less distressing for you if you can keep your vow."

"Good. I'm glad you support me in this."

"That's what sisters are for. Now, I talked to Anita Blackhorse this morning, and here's what she's thinking about doing. . . ."

Chapter Twelve

"**I** can't believe it's your birthday," Greta said to Tess on Friday. "Didn't you just have a birthday?"

"You're older than I am."

"Yes, but growing older bothers me less."

This was maddening but true.

"You sure you don't mind taking Belinda tonight?"

"Happy to do it," Greta said. "I figured the best present I could give you was some free time to do whatever you wanted to do until you get her back tomorrow morning."

Tess grinned, certain Greta was going to regret the offer long before morning. "I'm going to take a long bath—with loads of bubbles—and eat chocolate for dinner and watch an action flick on cable and read at least one completely escapist novel."

"An excellent plan."

When Tess picked Belinda up from school and told her the plan, she was equally delighted with it and happily packed pajamas and an armful of stuffed animals to bring to Greta's. Tess doubted that either Greta or Belinda would get much sleep, but that wasn't her problem—until morning.

She was on her way back home after dropping Belinda off, happily planning the order of events—dinner first, then bubble bath—when she saw a truck from Michael's shop parked at the curb next to her house.

What does he want? she wondered. He was probably going to yell at her for being such an insensitive jerk at the coffee shop. She squared her shoulders. She wasn't going to let him ruin her birthday. Not when she had plans.

She stopped short when she reached the porch. He was sitting on a glider and petting a dog. The glider didn't belong to her. The dog did.

"Hello, Michael," she said, brushing past him to put her key in the front door lock. "What are you doing here?"

"Delivering this piece of furniture." He gestured toward the glider. "Greta wanted to get you something great for your birthday and I suggested this. You said you wanted some lawn furniture."

Only the fact that he was talking a little too much, a little too fast, made her realize he was nervous.

"You made this?" Tess asked. Then she collected

herself and said, "Thank you. You delivered the piece of furniture. Do you need me to sign a delivery slip?"

"No."

She turned to face him, giving him a pointed look. "So?"

"I wanted to talk to you."

"I'm busy," she said.

"Yes, I know," he said. Then: "I told Greta I needed to talk to you. I asked her if she thought you would listen to me. She said that it depended."

"On what?"

"That's the curious thing," he said. "She said it depended on whether you had a blue heeler in the yard or not. And this little gal appears to be a blue heeler." The dog—Blue, not very creative, but Tess hadn't been the one to name her—thumped her tail emphatically on the porch floor.

"It's serial killers next," she snapped. "So talk."

"There you go. Greta was right. Who would have thought it hinged on a blue heeler? Will you come sit here? This is a great glider. I should know; I built it myself."

Reluctantly, Tess sat on the glider. Michael pushed off gently. She closed her eyes.

"Very nice," she said.

"I don't really know how to start," he said. "At first you just kept sneaking in under my defenses. And it was fine, I even enjoyed it, but I knew you'd push for the truth and I didn't want it to get that far. I didn't want to face the truth, and I didn't want you to learn it and then decide it reflected badly on me. I didn't want to lose you over it."

"So you got rid of me ahead of time," she said. "Very sensible, Michael."

"Greta warned me you were likely to be snappish."

"Why don't you and Greta go live happily ever after?"

"It's not Greta I want," he said calmly. "We'd turn each other into raving lunatics within two weeks."

"You've already turned me into a raving lunatic," Tess said, folding her arms across her chest.

"Which one of us went storming out of the coffee shop into the worst downpour of the century?" he inquired politely.

"You deserved it."

"Maybe." She could see the smile tug at his lips as he remembered. Then he sighed and said, "You were right. About my late wife. We had a volatile relationship. It had gotten worse and worse over the years but when she told me she was pregnant, I was ready to try harder than ever to fix our problems. But she—there's not an easy way to put this." He stopped and for once in her life, Tess didn't push. She waited quietly. After a while, he continued. "I wanted to try but my wife despised me as much as ever. During one of our last arguments, she told me the child—our son—wasn't mine. That I wasn't enough of a man to keep her, to keep any woman."

He paused and Tess unfolded her arms. She covered his hand with hers. His fingers curled over hers. "To be betrayed like that is—shattering," he said. "To be taunted about it is excruciating."

"I'm sorry," she said. "I know you would have loved that child no matter what. That you did love the child no matter what."

"I did. I wanted a family. I was willing to do almost anything to make it work." He stopped and didn't speak for a while. Then he sighed and said, "But even that she made into a weakness. That I would take another man's child into my heart and my life."

"So because you're a decent person and didn't send her packing, because you still wanted your family to work, and you were willing to take the child into your heart, she despised you even more?"

He didn't answer her but she didn't expect him to. She couldn't imagine how unspeakably painful it must have been.

"What did she mean by not being man enough for her?" she asked. "I don't get that." She moved a little closer to him. He shifted and put his arm around her shoulders and she nestled against his chest, hard and warm, safe and calm. She could feel his heart beating and she closed her eyes.

"I was never the kind of man she wanted," he said. "I choose not to fight. I told you I was a hockey player in college? I had enough talent to turn pro but I didn't because I don't have that internal conflict. If someone blocked one of my shots, my first reaction was to say, hey, good block. But a professional hockey player is supposed to react by wanting to beat up the opponent."

"I wondered about that," she said. "I noticed you have all your own teeth." She tucked her feet up under her. The rocking of the glider made her feel peaceful and relaxed.

"I don't feel the need to prove myself that way. I'm not the possessive or jealous type. If I love someone and she loves me, I'm willing to trust her. I don't have to demand to know where she is at all hours of the day. I don't have to accuse her of infidelity just because someone pays attention to her at a party. But my wife thought my behavior meant I didn't care about her."

"I always thought jealousy and possessiveness were destructive to relationships," Tess said. "Certainly they didn't help my marriage any. But she *wanted* that?"

"Apparently. I just wanted—peace, you know? Contentment, happiness. Home. She wanted drama and big emotional scenes."

"Was she very young?"

"Not that young," he said. "She wanted me to be more than a carpenter. It wasn't enough for her. She found it embarrassing when I'd attend a function with her and I wasn't a lawyer or a doctor or even something interesting like an epidemiologist."

"An epidemiologist?" Tess said, raising a brow. "But you like being a carpenter."

"I like being a carpenter."

"So she died before you could either get her to respect you for who you were or decide that her opinion wasn't a meaningful judgment."

"Something like that," he said.

"She must have been pretty unhappy with who she was. I'm sorry, Michael. It all sounds so sad." She traced her finger along his T-shirt, feeling the muscles respond to her touch. His heart started beating faster, but his voice was calm and even when he spoke.

"When you said that in the coffee shop, I was so angry. All these years I've been letting her make me unhappy. I was telling you not to listen to your family's judgments about who you are . . . and yet I was still listening to her judgments of me."

"It's complicated," Tess said.

"Except when it's simple," Michael said. "I love you. I want to be with you. And Belinda. And even the dogs."

She grinned. "Despite what my detractors say, I always knew I was your type."

He pulled a dark curl. "You're any man's type," he said.

She was going to respond but then she noticed something and asked, "Michael, did you paint this glider?"

"Yes. Why?"

"There's a menagerie in here. Little animals. I see a tiger and two bears on this arm." She reached across him and pointed.

"I thought Belinda would get a kick out of finding all the animals."

Tess turned to him, touching his face. "I knew it was

still in there somewhere," she said in satisfaction. "Your whimsical side. I love you, Michael Manning." Then she leaned over and kissed him with all her heart.

"Wow," he said sometime later. "You have never kissed me like that before."

"I haven't?"

"No. I'm pretty sure I would have remembered."

"I'll do better," she promised, leaning in for another kiss.

"No problem," Michael said and gave her that slow gentle smile.

WITHDRAWAL